# A Hood Affair

## A Novel By:

## Shmel Carter

## A Hood Affair

# Dedication

This book is dedicated to my father, Yarvin Sylvester Carter (R.I.P.) June 12, 1949-October 17, 2001. This is also dedicated to my cousin Dartanian "D" Counts 7/2/1979-02/28/1995.

May you R.I.P.

D, this poem is for you:

We were 15 years old when you died.

Those cowards took your life, and Dee we cried.

I remember it like yesterday.

My daddy, your uncle told me they took you away.

February 28 was a sad day.

Dee we love you, and you will forever be in our hearts.

No matter how much time passes your memory shall never part.

# Acknowledgments

First I want to thank my Savior, Lord Jesus Christ. Through him all things are possible. He spoke to me one day and said I have a talent and I need to use it. My kids A'Yana, Erica, and Eric Jr., I love y'all. You're the reason I breathe. Everything I do, I do it for you. You pushed me to do better. My beautiful aunt, Gwen Walker, I know you are shining down on me. Heaven got a beautiful angel in you. My aunt, Edna Ruth Carter, you are truly missed. Words can't even express how much. My great grandmother who died when I was 18, I was truly blessed to have my great grandmother around so long. My brother Darius, you are my number one fan. You have always pushed me over the years. I appreciate you more than you know. Thank you. My brother Quan, thank you just for being you. My sister Rasheda, keep on keeping on. My sister Ashley. I didn't forget about you. You might be far in distance, but you are near in heart. I love you and I hope one day we will be closer. My friend Teresa Miller, thank you for lending me your ear. I swear I needed those talks. Marquisha Kirklen, we are on our way. Just be patient. Crystal Davis, you are more than a cousin. I love you like a sister. Words cannot even express. If I make it you made it too. You already know that. Cathey White, we in there. The Carter family, there are too many of y'all to name. I love all of you. The Walker family, there's a lot of you too. I love y'all. My mom Claudette Walker, we are going to weather this storm together. I love you. My diva of a grandma, Dorothy Walker. You are truly the head of my family. Last but not least,

Jakatra Bell, you came back into my life and I swear it feels like you never left. We were teenage lovers and friends. It feels so good to have my friend back. I now believe there are still some real men left in this world. You're my lover, my best friend, and I love you dearly. My CMC Mercy Patient Registration family. I love y'all dearly. Lakiedra Davis, my cousin, I love you dearly. Rashun Hill, we have been friends since junior high school. Those Ranson Raiders days. We fall out, but everyone knows not to get in our business. Valencia Frazier, my big sister. You came late in my life, but you're so bubbly and I love you for just being you. My grandma Flora Carter. I was a little girl when you died. I can't believe the stories my cousins tell about you (lol.) I keep saying not my sweet grandma. Gertrude McCormick, you are my grandma. I never felt anything different. You were a beautiful person inside and out and may you R.I.P. Kancham Potts, I still remember your spirit. You will always be in my heart. May you R.I.P. Cynthia "Lynn" Hill, my big cousin. I admire you more than you know. You have overcome all obstacles. I have to keep shouting out my girls. Crystal Davis, you already know. Marquisha, we are going to Paris. I know if I don't mention Jakatra Bell's name again he will have a fit. Ursula McClary, welcome to our crazy family. I hope you are ready. Venita Smart, I still love you girl. My nephew who was my first child, Darius Walker Jr. Your aunt is so proud of you right now. I am really starting to see that young man that I knew you could be. Ghetto Princess Publishing, we are going to take the world by storm. Cheryl Nicholson, Joyvonna Ham, Bryan Graves, Janise Zayas, Avon Foley, my second shift crew at Carolinas Healthcare

System Mercy, thank you for putting up with me. I love

y'all to pieces. If I left anybody out, I'm sorry. I will

remember you on my next book. Don't be mad at me.

# Chapter 1

## Neicee

*Ring. Ring. Ring.*

Looking over at the clock, I saw it read 3:30 a.m. and someone decided to call my house. I also noticed Q, my no-good boyfriend, was not home. *Who in the world is calling me at this time of morning?* Igorning the ringing phone, I rolled over and tried to go back to sleep. "Take a Bow" by Rihanna was the next song I heard, which meant my cell phone was ringing. That was Q's ringtone, so I answered the phone with an attitude.

"Nigga where you at this time of morning, since you ain't home?" Was the words that left my mouth.

"Neicee calm down. This Tone. Q been shot," he informed me. Hearing those words, it was as if all the air had been sucked out my body.

"What happened Tone?" I asked franticly. All kinds of thoughts were running through my mind. I was just accusing Q of all kinds of things and my man had been shot. I felt so bad.

"Just get to Carolina Medical Center and I'll explain everything when you get here."

"Is it serious Tone?" I needed as much information as I could about Q's condition. I needed to know what I was walking into.

"He gon' live girl." I breathed a sigh of relief when he said that. "Now get over here. Don't be taking all damn day either, because I know you." With that, he hung up before I could respond.

Jumping out of bed, I began to get dressed. I still had to represent my man by looking my best, so I did a quick wash up and brushed my teeth. I put on a red one-piece Baby Phat dress and threw on my white Baby Phat thong sandals. I then combed out my fresh doobie and threw on some Mac lip-gloss. Grabbing the keys to my fully loaded 2011 sky blue Mercedes-Benz SL class convertible, I headed out the door. Once I was in, I pushed the button on my dashboard to let the top down. It wasn't too hot or too cold; the weather was just right for May.

As I pulled out the driveway, I looked around our neighborhood. I was happy with the lifestyle we lived. We stayed in Ballantyne, a very upscale neighborhood. The house was in my name because I was a high-priced lawyer while Q was a high-priced drug dealer. Imagine that, the lawyer and the drug dealer.

That is how I met Q; I was representing one of his homeboys. Q hired me because I was the baddest bitch in Charlotte NC, and hadn't lost a case yet. His boy was charged with the murders of two drug dealers, and I got him off. After the trial was over, that was when Q stepped to me.

"Hey Ms. Shaneice Love. What do I owe you for this?" he asked me.

"You don't owe me anything. You have already paid your bill. It's my job to defend and win. Excuse me," I told him as I tried to walk around him.

He grabbed my arm and prevented me from doing so. "Let me take you to lunch or something. Don't be trying to act like that. You know you want some of this thug loving," he teased.

He couldn't see me from the way our body was positioned, but I was grinning real hard. He was a sexy chocolate nigga with a sexy bald head, and in each ear was a diamond stud. Q reminded me a lot of the actor Omar Epps, and he was wearing the hell out of that Armani suit.

Turning around to face him, I said, "Mr. Dupree I would love to have lunch with you." I wasn't going to even lie, I was feeling his ass.

"Quentin," he corrected me.

"Huh?"

"My name is Quentin, but you can call me Q. All my friends do."

"Well Q you can call me Neicee. All my friends do," I informed him.

We'd been inseparable since then.

My stroll down memory lane ended when I pulled into the emergency room parking lot. There were a lot of cars there so I assumed the ER was real busy being that it was 5:15 in the morning on a Saturday. I guess the clubs were packed last night.

I walked into the ER and was greeted by Tone.

"Neicee you didn't have to get dressed up to come to the damn hospital. Your man just got shot and you at home getting all dolled up and shit."

"You told me he was going to live, so I didn't think it was that serious," I explained to him.

"I said he was going to live, and he is. That still ain't mean you had to take your time." I followed him to the waiting room as he ranted on. "He in surgery. He got shot in the leg and they're trying to get the bullet out. He gon' be a'ight though."

"What happened Tone? You still ain't told me what happened, and did you call his mama?"

"You know I called Alexis. She's here. She went downstairs to the cafeteria. We were at Club Nox and he caught a stray bullet. I'm still gon' see that nigga that did it though," Tone explained as he bobbed his head up and down.

"Just leave it alone Tone. It could have happened to anybody. Y'all was at the wrong place at the wrong time, and just like you said it was a stray bullet."

I looked up just as Alexis was walking into the room with Q's little sister, Monique, at her side. They both came and sat beside me and Tone.

"Hey y'all," I said to them.

"Hey Neicee. I knew you would be here by now, so I bought you a cup of French vanilla cappuccino," said Q's mother.

"Thank you."

"The family of Quentin Dupree," the doctor walked in and said just as the words left my mouth. We all stood up and walked to him.

Alexis was the first to speak first. "How is my son doing Doctor?" she asked.

"He's doing great and the surgery was a success. He is highly sedated so he has not woken up just yet. The bullet hit him in the leg, so he will have crutches for a while. He doesn't need to put a lot of pressure on his leg and we'll be keeping him here for a few days for observation," the doctor clarified to us all.

"Can we see him?" I wanted to know.

"Yes, you can see him for a few minutes, but he needs some rest."

"Thank you doctor," we all said as he walked out the room.

We walked into Q's room, and he was laying there looking so peaceful with his right leg wrapped up. Alexis walked over to his bed and kissed him on the cheek, followed by his sister. Tone stood back quietly, and I kissed him on the lips.

"Neicee, now that I know Quentin is okay I'm going to head on home. I'll come back later on in the evening."

"Okay Alexis I'm gon' stay though. I want to be here when he wakes up."

Tone gave me a hug and told me he was out too and would be back also.

I was going through my iPhone on the pull out chair when I heard someone whispering my name. I looked up and Q was looking at me with his eyes half closed. Getting up, I walked over to him.

"Hey baby," I said to him. He reached out for my hand to pull me closer. "You scared me Q. I'm glad you okay."

"I only got shot in the leg, Neicee. I'm gon' be okay, but I'm gon' see that nigga though," he stated weakly.

"You sound just like Tone, and y'all need to let it go. It was a stray bullet. It could have happened to anybody." I noticed the look on Q's face when I repeated what Tone said. Something about the way he was looking led me to believe there was more to the story than they were sharing, but I left it alone. I didn't want to start no drama in the hospital, because knew I could get ghetto when provoked.

"You been here all this time Neicee?" Q asked, changing the subject.

"Yes, you know I couldn't leave you. I had to be here when you woke up. Your mom and sister were here too. They said they'll come back and Tone said he would too."

"Get Tone on the phone for me Neicee."

I did as I was told and got Tone on the phone. Handing the phone to Q, I walked out the room to give him some privacy. I went to the waiting room and called my best friend, Na Na. There was more to Q's story, and I knew he was lying. Q knew I was straight hood. Hell, I was born and raised in the projects. I just overcame and got out.

Na Na answered on the first ring. "I was wondering when you was gon' call me and tell me what happened to Q. I thought I was your best friend and I have to hear from the neighborhood hood rat, Maya, that Q was shot," Na-Na fussed.

"I was gon' tell you. I been at this hospital since about five this morning. What did Maya say happened? I know it's more to the story than what Tone and Q is saying. I love Q, but I ain't stupid. I know he is a ho." I wouldn't be surprised if this had something to do with another chick.

"Girl, she didn't really say much. All she said was some stuff jumped off at the club and Q got shot. What do you think happened Neicee?"

"I don't know but the reason I'm tripping is because they want to get this nigga so bad. If it was a stray bullet, they would drop it. That tells me they know who it was. All I know is, it better not have been over a trick, because I'm about tired of Q's shit."

"Well if you want me to, I'll confront Tone's ass because I'm tired of him too. If I find out he fucking Maya I got something for both they asses. She be waltzing past him like everything cool. I'm trying to be cool because I don't want our daughter to see me act a fool."

I laughed when she said that.

"Girl you crazy. Let me get off this phone. I got to go back and check on Q. Where is Tone because I just called him for Q?"

"He stepped outside when Q called."

"Oh, a'ight then Na Na. I'll hit you up later," I said then hung up.

When I got back to the room, Q was watching TV so I sat at the foot of the bed. "I'm going to head home, take me a shower, and get a little bit of rest. You seem to be okay so I will be back later on today."

"Yeah, whatever Neicee." He had the nerve to sound as if he had an attitude.

I looked at him like he had lost his mind.

"What do you mean by that Q? I ain't done a damn thing to you, so you better take it out on that bitch you got fucked up over last night." I let his ass know.

"I didn't get fucked up over a bitch, so you don't know what you talking about. I was waiting on this, and personally I don't want to hear the bullshit."

"I don't give a damn what you want to hear, because you gon' hear it! I put up with your bullshit all the time. No, I ain't never caught you but I know you cheat. I ain't no fool! When I do catch your ass, it's gon' be a bad day for both of you because I have put three years into this relationship. All I said to you was I will be back later and you caught an attitude. With all that said, I will be back later." I was heated as I walked out the room, and if I could've, I would've slammed the damn door.

My phone was ringing before I could even get to my car and I knew it was Q because of the ringtone. I sent his ass right to the voicemail and hopped in my car. Before I could pull out the parking lot he had sent me a text message.

*I'm sorry Neicee u right I shldnt be takn nothn out on u got a lot on my mind.*

I pulled out the lot and headed home without responding. I turned the radio on to Power 98 and listened to "Take You Down" by Chris Brown.

# Chapter 2

## Q

I pushed the button on the morphine dripper because my leg was hurting really bad. I shouldn't have gone off on Neicee like that when she ain't done nothing to me. Things were just fucked and I wasn't messing with that bitch Leeka no more; she was the reason my ass got shot.

I don't know why I was even tripping because I saw her with that nigga. Shit, I wasn't even feeling her like that anyways. It was more of my pride in the way, if anything. I let that nigga catch me slipping since I had my guard down while arguing with that bitch. Next thing I knew, I heard gunfire and I got shot in the leg. I was gon' see that punk ass nigga she messed with though.

Neicee wasn't stupid; she knew when my ass was lying. I loved that girl 'til the death of me, and I didn't know why I kept cheating on her. It was starting to catch up to me now. Those girls were getting crazy, wanting me to move in with them and shit, knowing I had a live-in already. All of them were crazy; I wasn't leaving Neicee for nobody.

Neicee was bad as hell with beauty and brains, and Beyoncé ain't have shit on my baby. She had an hourglass shape, and her butt was so firm you could put a glass on it and it wouldn't fall. Her breasts sat up without a bra, and she had the prettiest feet I'd ever seen. Neicee kept herself together and stayed in the hair and nail salon every week. My boo was a freak in the bedroom too, always aiming to please me; that's why I had no clue why I cheated on her.

Hearing a knock at the door, I told whoever it was to come in.

Speaking of this ho, Leeka walked in. I'm glad Neicee had already left, because Leeka would have been laying in the hospital too. All these hos knew

Neicee would fuck them up so they didn't get too froggy.

"Hey baby," she greeted as she walked over and tried to kiss me.

I turned my head. I didn't let them hos kiss me in my mouth. Neicee was the only one that could kiss me. She started laughing because she knew the deal.

"Girl what you doing here? You know if Neicee catch you in here she gon' fuck both of us up."

"Fuck Neicee! You the only one scared of her. She ain't gon' do shit to me."

"Yeah, whatever. You know Neicee will fuck you up; don't play. And I ain't scared of her, I just don't want to lose her, especially not over you," I said in a serious tone. I wanted her to know that I was dead ass serious.

"Fuck you Q. I ain't trying to be with you."

I waved her off because I wasn't trying to hear that shit. Plus, I knew she was lying anyways.

"You know your nigga is on my list. I'm gon' see him so he better be hiding."

"I ain't got nothing to do with that; that's between y'all. I don't even fuck with that nigga like that anyways, so I don't know why he was tripping. He brought this on himself because he knew better. He knew when he shot you he should have killed you. That's why he ran when he realized you was only hit in the leg. Tone was firing on him though," she explained. "Well I see you ain't dying so I'm gon' roll up out of here. I just came to check on you."

"A'ight Leeka, make this the last time you contact me. I ain't fucking with you like that no more."

"Oh you ain't fucking with me no more? You ain't fucking with me no more Q? You an asshole. You gon' get what's coming to you. All them nights you was fucking me and now you gon' say it's over. I don't think so. You fucked with the wrong bitch this time." At that time Tone walked in. He grabbed Leeka and took her out of my room and returned back shortly.

"What was that about Q?" he asked once he walked in and took a seat.

"I told that bitch I ain't fucking with her no more and she went crazy. I ain't worried about her. I got to make it right with Neicee. Fuck those hos."

"Man, I feel what you saying because I ain't fucking with Maya no more either. That ho crazy too. Well enough of that bullshit, I came to tell you I know where that nigga Ron at. Whenever you ready to roll we can handle him or I can roll solo."

"Nah nigga, I want in on that action. The doctor don't have to release me, because I am releasing myself in the morning. All I want is some pain medicine."

"A'ight my nigga I'm out. I'll see you then." He gave me some dap and he left.

# Neicee

I was knocked out in my bed when the alarm sounded. I had set it because I only wanted to sleep for only two hours so I could get back to the hospital with Q. Yeah he had pissed me off and though I loved him, I was really tired of his shit. He stayed out all night and some nights he didn't even bother to come home, at all. Shit, I ain't Super Woman; I got feelings too and he fail to realize that.

Q didn't know it but I would go through his phone and see all kinds of text messages in there. See, I knew all about his hos; Leeka, Santeria, and Dee-Dee. I never confronted his ass about it because I wanted to catch him in the act. I knew my man and once I stepped to him about those texts he would run some bullshit lie about how he let his homeboy use his phone. So to avoid hearing that, I decided to not even waste my breathe. Even dealing with all Q's B.S, he never seen me shed a tear behind him for the simple fact that I didn't want him to know he had broken me down. I loved Q and there was no denying that, but I wasn't gon' keep playing the fool. Either he was going to get his shit together or I was leaving him for good.

I got up out my bed and walked into my bathroom, and admired the scene before me. Standing in the doorway, I looked around and smiled at the painting on the wall. Anybody that knew me knew I had a thing for Dolphins, and that is exactly what I had painted on my walls. I looked over at my Jacuzzi tub. I wouldn't mind relaxing in it, but I knew I didn't have the time. I opted for the stand alone shower instead.

Stripping out of my clothes, I took a shower and once I was done, I brushed my teeth. I couldn't walk around with morning breath even though it was in the afternoon. I went to my huge walk-in closet and looked around. We had so many clothes between the both of us we had to have two. I couldn't really decide what to put on, so I grabbed my black Diesel jumper dress, pulled out my red Prada pumps, some red earrings and my red matching bracelets to go with it. Once I grabbed my red Prada purse and shades, I began getting dressed. Being that I didn't wear any make-up, I just applied my Mac lip gloss, and looked in my full length mirror. Once I saw that I looked good I headed out the door.

When I walked in Q's room he was sitting up watching TV. When he turned it off and turned to look at me, I prepared myself for another battle.

"Hey sexy. You wearing the hell out of that dress. You gon' make me pull you in this hospital bed and tell the nurses do not disturb," He jokingly said. I laughed as I walked over to the bed and sat down.

"You silly Q," I said as I pulled the covers off of him. I pulled the hospital gown up and started stroking his dick before putting his entire manhood in my mouth then started deep throating it. I heard a moan escape his mouth and it made me go harder. I knew my head game was tight and hell, he even knew it as well.

Q was moaning as if he didn't have a care in the world while I was making slurping sounds with my mouth. My saliva was flowing down his shaft as I sucked harder and just as he was about to cum, I pulled him out my mouth and began jerking him off. Grabbing the towel he had next to the bed, I cleaned him up.

"That's why I love you baby, because you're a freak. You know how to make a nigga feel good no matter the situation." Just as the word left Q's mouth the doctor walked in.

"How are you feeling Mr. Dupree?" he asked.

"I'm a'ight Doc. I'm ready to get outta here and get home to my lady." The doctor looked at me when Q made that comment and gave me a smile.

"You will be out of here soon. Are you having any pain?"

"Yeah my leg hurts, but I'm straight. When can I go home? If you don't release me by the morning I'm releasing myself. I got things to do." I didn't know what Q had to do that was so important that he just had to get home, but I knew it wasn't because of me. I didn't care what he had just said.

"Well Mr. Dupree I do want you to stay for a few days but if you insist I will release you in the morning. I'll write you a prescription for pain and see you in the morning." With that being said, he walked out the room.

Looking over at Q, I said, "Well it looks like you're getting out of here in the morning. I don't have to be in court tomorrow and I don't have any clients to see so I will be at your beck and call." I smiled.

"Make sure you be here early. I ain't trying to be here no longer than I have to."

"Where's your car at Q?" He hadn't mentioned his car and it's not like him to just leave it anywhere unsupervised.

"It should be on the West Side. Tone drove it to him and Na Na's spot."

"Oh okay." I said. "Have your mom and sister been back up here?"

"No, but she called. I told her not to come up here. Tone did drop by though."

"Did anybody else drop in?" I asked as I eyed him suspiciously. I was just trying to see had any of his hos been.

"Neicee will you go get me some real food? You can go to the cafeteria. I don't really care, but they ain't feeding a nigga in here," he said, totally ignoring my question. I was going to let him have that lil bit, only because I didn't feel like arguing with his ass.

"Yeah," was all I said as I got up and headed to the door.

As I was getting on the elevator it felt like someone was watching me. I turned and looked around but didn't see anyone. I was beginning to feel weird so I hurried to get Q's food so I could get back to the room where he was.

When I got back to the room, I handed Q his food and watched him demolish it. He barely spoke two words as he at his three slices of pizza and chili cheese fries. Once he was done, I stood and gently kissed his lips.

"Q I'm gon' get on out of here. I'll be back early in the morning to pick you up and I'll bring you some more clothes when I come."

"A'ight baby. Call me when you get in to let me know you got in safe." Once I gave Q another kiss, left out the room and heading home. I didn't know what was wrong but I did know something wasn't right and I wanted to get home where I knew I would be safe.

# *Chapter 3*

## *Neicee*

As I was pulling into the driveway of my home, my cell phone rang. Being that it was playing *"Love in the Club"* by Usher, I knew it was a private or blocked number so I didn't bother to answer it. I usally didn't answer those on my personal phone so I politely sent the caller to the voicemail. As I was stepping out my car, it bagan to ring again and just like the first time, I sent the caller to the voicemail once again. This time around they left a voicemail and when I checked it, the idoit was just breathing through the phone. *Ignorant Bastard.*

It seemed that as soon as I stepped foot in the door, my house phone begin ringing. Running into the kitchen, I grabbed the cordless phone off the cradle and answered it.

"Hello," I said.

"Neicee I thought I told you to call me when you got in the house," Q roared from the other end of the phone.

"My fault Q. I was getting ready to. I had actually just want through the door."

"Well I still need to know that you're okay Neicee. You should've called me when you pulled into the driveway."

"Since when Q? Why are you so concerned about me being okay all of a sudden? What's going on?" With him acting all concerned and that person calling my phone, I wondered if he knew what was going on.

"Nothing. Just make sure you're here early to pick me up. I love you girl. Remember that no matter what comes our way I love you." I don't know if it has something to do with him being shot or what, but Q was acting strange.

"I love you too Q… I love you too." I said right before we ended the call.

The phone rang again and being that I thought it was Q, I answered without looking at the caller ID.

"Hey baby. You calling back already," I said with a big smile on my face. I was taken aback by the operator.

"This is a prepaid call. You will not be charged for this call. This call is from a federal prisoner. Peanut."

*Peanut*, I repeated to myself. How in the world did he get my number? Peanut was my ex-boyfriend. He got locked up while I was in college and was sentenced to ten years. Judging by my calculations he should have about two more years before he's released.

"Press five to accept." I pressed five.

"Hello," I stuttered.

"Hey Ne Ne." Peanut had always called me that since I could remember. He said that was his nickname for me because he didn't want to call me what everybody else called me. That was understandable back in the days when we were together.

"Hey Peanut. How did you get my number?"

"I got my ways Ne Ne. I ain't heard from you in about three years. I thought we was better than that."

"Peanut the last time I came to see you I told you I was moving on. You agreed with me and told me not to wait for you," I refreshed his memory.

"Yeah I did, but I thought you would still drop a nigga a letter or visit or something."

"I put money on your books every month. I know you didn't think your so-called friends be doing it."

"Nah I didn't think that Ne Ne. I knew it was you. I was hoping it was anyway," he said with a chuckle. "The reason I'm calling is because I'm about to get out soon and I need a place to lay my head."

"From my calculations Peanut you got about two more years." Shit, he had plenty of time to find a spot to lay his head.

"Nah you know I only have to do 85% percent and I'm almost done with that. Plus that new drug bill passed. You already know that though Ms. Lawyer. That helped me out a lot too so I gotta do about six months in the halfway house."

"Peanut you can't stay with me. I got a man." I had to go ahead and throw that shit out there. I already knew that's what he was thinking because he called me.

"I'll put you up in something until you get straight, though." That was the least I could do for him. He'd always looked out for me when we were younger so I wasn't about to just leave him helpless.

"A'ight ma, you got it like that. You can put a nigga up?"

"You know I got you Peanut. You good for it. I can't let Q find out though, because he would flip out and you can't be calling my house phone. Let me give you my cell number and you can put that one on your list. You got to take my house phone off," I said while shaking my head as if he could actually see me.

"A'ight I ain't trying to get nothing popping with you and your nigga, so I'm gon' respect that. I will put your celly on my list and take your house number off. Aye, this phone 'bout to hang up so I'll hit you once your cell number clear." Just as he said that, the phone hung up and I sat it back on the reciever.

Going upstairs to my bathroom, I ran me a bath and turned on the jets in the Jacuzzi. While I waited on the tub to fill I put my iPod in the dock. I wanted to hear some old school music so I put Monica and Xscape on repeat. I grabbed the cordless and my personal cell phone and headed back to the bathroom.

After my bath I decided to call my oldest brother Lamont. Being that I'm the only girl out of six kids and the youngest, they gave all my boyfriends a hard time. I honestly didn't know how they feel about Q, though, because they never really said anything. I did know, that had they known the bullshit he takes me through, they would surely fuck him up.

When I got Lamont's voicemail, I left a message then decided to call my second oldest brothe,r Damon. He picked up on the first ring.

"What's up li'l sis?" He said.

"Nothing much. I was just calling to check on you. I hadn't talked to you in a while. You know Q got shot," I got straight to the point.

"Nah I didn't know that. What happened?" As I told my brother what happened I could hear my oldest brother Lamont in the background.

"Ask Lamont why he didn't answer his phone when I called. It could have been life or death and he left me hanging," I said jokingly. I heard Damon telling him and Lamont was telling him he was just getting ready to hit me back. I talked to my brothers for a little while and I hung up.

I was flipping through the channels and decided on a Lifetime movie. They always show good movies on Sunday. I also decided to call and check on Q once I got comfortable.

"What's up baby?" he said as he answered the phone.

"Nothing, I was just calling to check on you," I said as I slid my hand down between my legs. I didn't know why but I was feeling a little freaky. "I want you to tell me what you would do to me if you was here, because I'm horny." He chuckled when I said that.

"You horny, huh? I wonder what I can do about that. Why don't you just come over to the hospital and ride your dick. He miss you too."

"Don't tempt me Q. I can wait though, because I'm gon' put it on you tomorrow. I'm gon' be at the hospital bright and early."

"You do that," he said.

"A'ight baby I will see you in the morning," I told him and I hung up.

My cell phone started to ring again. It was a private number again. I knew it wasn't Peanut because he

couldn't have had my cell on his list this quick. I just
ignored it and sent it to voicemail.

The next morning I got up bright and early and
washed up. After getting Q something to wear, I headed
out the door. I knew Q was going to need room so I
decided to drive our Escalade truck. He hadn't been
gone long but I missed his ass so much and couldn't
wait for him to come home.

# Q

I looked at my cell phone and it read 9:30 in the morning. The doctor had just left and released me as promised. Leeka had been blowing my phone up all morning but I wasn't about to even entertain her ass. I already had to call her and go off on her last night with the bullshit she text me when Neicee left. Stupid bitch talking about some she saw my bitch getting on the elevator and she better watch her back. That's when her ass hit me with that *I'm pregnant* bullshit.

I used protection every time and I ain't never went up in her raw. If she was pregnant it damn sho' wasn't mine. I had a psycho bitch on my hands but if she did anything to Neicee she'll be dead and I put that on everything I love.

"Hey baby," Neicee said as she walked in the door. She came right in helping me get dressed. When she turned her back to me, I turned my cell phone off on the low.

"What's up? I'm so glad to see you," I said as I buzzed the nurse in. I was ready to get the fuck out of this place.

We passed Leeka in the hallway when we were leaving and she was eyeballing us to death. What the fuck her ass was doing here, I didn't know. I was just glad Neicee didn't know what she looked like. I thought I was gon' piss on myself when I saw her ass. Neicee didn't pay her any attention. She said she was used to girls staring at me. I don't really know if she trusted me or if she was just tired of me.

Neicee helped me up the stairs when we got home. As I was lying across the bed she came in the room with a small tub of soapy water.

"I know you can't get the dressing on your leg wet, so I'm gon' wash you up," Neicee said.

After my wash up Neicee started caressing my dick. She took it all in with one big swallow. I grabbed her hair while her head bobbed her head up and down my dick. She was laying it on real thick. My eyes started rolling in the back of my head. I forgot all about the pain in my leg. I turned her over so I could return the favor, but she stopped me.

"It's all about you baby. Just relax and enjoy. I stuck my finger in her pussy and then put my finger in my mouth.

"You taste real good."

Her pussy was dripping wet. She climbed on top of me and slid her pussy down over my dick. She hadn't been with but one other dude, so her pussy was good and tight. She started clamping her pussy muscles on my dick and I was about to lose my fucking mind. She was riding like she was at a rodeo then she turned around and started riding me backwards. She was laying on her stomach bouncing her fat ass up and down on my dick and I started bucking back at her.

"Oh shit, baby, I'm getting ready to cum girl." Q announced

"Come on Q. This your pussy. I'ma come with you daddy." When my baby said that, I bust a big nut all in her. If she was ovulating she had plenty of sperm to choose from.

# Chapter 4

## Neicee

I laid on my back exhausted from having sex with Q. I guess he thought I was stupid. I knew he turned his cell phone off because I peeped it when he was in the bathroom.

"Dang Q your phone ain't ring all day. What you do, tell the fellas you was spending the day with me and not to disturb you?" I decided to play his little game with him.

"Nah I ain't tell them niggas nothing. I don't have to answer to them; they answer to me. They probably still think I'm in the hospital but Tone can handle them anyway."

Speaking of Tone, my cell phone started ringing. It was playing "What About Your Friends" by TLC. I knew it was Na Na.

"What's up girl?" I asked her as I answered the phone.

"Nothing, I was calling you for Tone. He said to ask Q why he got his phone off." I couldn't wait to hear his answer.

Looking over at him, I said, "Q, Tone wanna know why you got your phone off."

"I ain't got my phone off. My battery must be dead or something." He flat out lied. I knew it was a damn lie because Q never just let his phone die like that.

"Well charge it up and call Tone," I said with a roll of my eyes. "A'ight Na Na, I'll holla at you later girl."

# Q

I was gon' get Tone for calling me out like that.
Now I had to turn my phone back on. I hoped Leeka's
crazy ass didn't start calling and sending text messages.

"What's up Tone?" I said with a bit of frustration.

"Not much. I was just wondering did you still
want one of the boys to handle that pick up?"

"Yeah man. I had forgot all about that. It's so
much stuff going on and tell D-Dot to handle that and
hit me when he get back in town." As I was saying that,
my line beeped. Looking at the screen, I saw it was
Leeka so I ignored it.

"A'ight Q, I'll holla at you later."

"Yeah that's what's up." I hung up the phone. I decided against turning my phone off this time because I didn't want to look suspicious so I just left it alone. I looked over at Neicee. She was flipping through the TV channels.

# *Chapter 6*

## *Neicee*

Q was a stupid nigga if he thought I was stupid. It was funny to me when Na Na called. He was talking about his battery must be dead. He still hadn't put the phone on the charger. I wasn't sweating it though, because I was getting ready to start doing me.

I got out the bed to walk to the room I used for my study. I wanted to get on the computer. I wasn't worried about Q disturbing me. He would take a minute to get there because of his leg.

"Where you going Neicee?"

"In the study. I want to surf the Internet."

"Oh. Will you make me something to eat when you get through?"

"Yeah," I said and walked out the room. The first thing I did on the Internet was go to bop.gov, the federal website where you can check release dates for federal prisoners. I put in Darnell Phillips. I wanted to check on Peanut and see what it said his release date was. When I pulled it up it still had a release date of 2017. I didn't understand, because why would Peanut lie? I guess they hadn't updated it yet. I would just ask him when he called. Next I went on Facebook to see if I had any messages. I had a few from a couple of guys who were telling me how sexy I was. I smiled because I got a kick out of some of the messages. I responded back to them. One of the messages was from a guy in Charlotte. His screen name was "Dark Sexy." Looking at his pictures the name fit. I had never seen him in person, but I'd been chatting with him on here for a while. I was thinking about taking him up on his offer if Q kept tripping. He seemed okay. The only problem is where would we go? Everybody knew I was Q's girl. I guess we would have to go to Concord ,NC. His message stated he was still waiting on me. I typed him a message back: *I know you are. I might have to take you up on your offer real soon.* I closed Facebook just as Q was calling my name.

I stuck my head in our bedroom door to see what he wanted.

"Did you forget about my food Neicee?"

"No," I said with an attitude as I walked out the room. I walked down the back staircase into the kitchen. I didn't really feel like cooking so I cooked him four hotdogs and some fries.

# *Chapter 7*

## Q

I reached for my phone as it let off a text message alert. I looked at it. It was that damn Leeka. That girl just didn't stop.

Leeka: *Q I don't know y u tripping I hope u ready to be a daddy.*

I hit delete on my iPhone. That girl was crazy. I ain't saying she wasn't pregnant, but it couldn't have been mine. Neicee walked in with my plate.

"Why you ain't cook boo? You know I love your cooking."

"I ain't feel like it. I gotta be in court all day tomorrow."

# Neicee

I walked toward the night stand on my side of the bed. My Galaxy Note 5 was ringing. That was my work phone. I picked it up.

"Hello."

"Shaneice this Mike. They brought me in for questioning. I'm downtown. Can you come down here?"

Mike was one of my best clients. I had gotten him off of a drug charge and plenty of misdemeanors. He paid me real good and had me on retainer. He paid me in advance because he never knew when he was gon' need me.

"What's the charge Mike?"

"They trying to say I murdered a cop."

"I'm on my way." I hung up the phone. Q was looking at me when I got off the phone.

"I gotta go see a client. I will be back when I'm done. If you need anything just call me." I walked over and gave him a juicy kiss on the lips. He slapped my butt. I grabbed my keys and headed out the door.

When I got to the jail I walked to the desk. I told the officer behind the desk who I was and who I was there to see. She sent me to the interrogation room. I heard Mike through the door.

"I told you I ain't kill no cop."

I knocked on the door and a police officer opened it.

"I'm Shaneice Love. I'm representing Mike Young."

"What kind of evidence do you have on my client? If you're going to charge him for murder then charge him so I can get started on his bail. If not then let him go."

"Hi Ms. Love. I'm Detective Smith. I've heard a lot about you. I brought your client in for questioning. Someone dropped us a hint that your client killed an undercover cop."

"Detective Smith, do you have any evidence against my client?"

"No, not as this time, but I know he did it. I'm gon' make it my personal business to bring him down." He was saying all this while laying pictures on the table. "This is Detective Hill. He was a good friend of mine. I am the godfather to his kids. As you know I can hold him for 48 hours, but I ain't gon' do that."

I looked the detective dead in his eyes.

"I am not intimated by anything you just said. My reputation precedes me. I'm the baddest bitch in Charlotte. You can do what you feel, but I will tear everything you bring down in court. You say you ain't gon' hold my client so you have a good day. Come on Mike." I walked out the room with a swagger that would stop traffic. Mike looked at me and smiled.

"That's why you my lawyer."

"Mike I don't know what's going on or what happened. I want to see you in my office tomorrow around 2:30. We need to go over some things so I will be ready for Detective Smith."

"That's cool Neicee. I will be there. I got some things to discuss with you anyway."

We both walked off. I went to my car. I don't know where Mike went, because the police brought him there. Knowing how he rolled though I'm sure he had some broad there waiting on him. I mostly took a lot of drug dealer cases. I didn't like taking rape cases, because I wasn't about losing. If I felt like the rapist was guilty I didn't want to be responsible for putting them back out on the streets. I hopped in my car and pulled off.

My cell phone was ringing from a private number again. This was really starting to get on my nerves.

"Hello." No answer. I hung up. Not even two minutes later my text alert went off.

Unknown: *U r a dead bitch. U better watch ur back.*

It was from a blocked number. I didn't know what's going on. I didn't do any dirt. I had fucked a few girls up over the years, but nothing bad enough for someone to want to kill me. I wondered who hated me that much. I wasn't gon' worry about it though. I could handle my own. I was the youngest of five boys and as rough as they came.

I was pulling in my garage by now. I grabbed my stuff and got out the car.

# Chapter 8

## Q

I was on the phone arguing with Leeka. I didn't even hear Neicee come in the house. I had just told Leeka if she was pregnant then she needed to get a fucking abortion because the baby wasn't mine. I looked up and saw Neicee looking at me with hate in her eyes. I didn't know how much of the conversation she heard, but I knew I was busted. I hung up the phone on Leeka. "Hey baby," I said. She didn't say anything though. She just turned and walked out the door.

I couldn't run after her, because my leg was fucked up. I knew I had fucked up and I didn't know how to fix it.

# Neicee

Q must've taken me for a motherfucking joke. I heard his whole conversation with that ho Leeka. He was so caught up with arguing with her he didn't even notice me. I was standing there for like ten minutes before he even looked up. All I could think about was that she might be pregnant with his baby. I couldn't take that. I loved Q and the thought alone just tore my heart in two. I needed time to think. I still had my condo downtown, but I wasn't leaving my house. I wasn't giving no bitch that satisfaction. I would just move into one of the guest rooms until I figured out what was going on.

I picked up the phone to call Na Na. She answered on the third ring.

"What's up girl?" she said to me. I began to tell her what I just walked in on.

"Oh no Neicee. Do you want to come over here for a few days?"

"No Na Na, I'm straight. Q will know to look for me there. I ain't leaving my house. I'ma just go on and stay in one of the guest bedrooms for a while."

"Okay it's your choice. I'm here if you need me." We hung up.

By this time Q was calling my phone. I knew he thought I left the house, but I never did. Our house was so big that he didn't know I was in the other room. I sent him to voicemail. I didn't feel like being bothered right now.

The sound of my work phone woke me up. It was already morning. I had no idea that I was in the guest room that long. I looked at the time on my phone. I had an hour and a half to be in court. It would take me every bit of that to get ready, but I had to cut that time in half. I ran down to my bedroom. Q was sitting in the bed. He don't look like he had gotten any sleep. I really didn't care though. He just looked at me. I ran to the bathroom and hopped in the shower. I put on my grey Armani suit and some black Jimmy Choo Mary Jane pumps. I pulled my hair back into a ponytail. My hair was really long. It reached down to the middle of my back. It was all mine too; no hair extensions.

As I was grabbing my pocketbook Q called my name.

"Neicee we need to talk."

"Not right now Q. I'm about to be late for court."

I pulled into the parking garage off of 4th Street. I was hoping there were some parking spots close by, because I was pushing it. I had about twenty minutes to get to the courtroom and I still needed to talk to my client before he went to trial. I needed to tell him what to expect. Today was the first day of trial.

He was a 19-year-old kid who was charged with being the getaway driver for a bank robbery. He came from a good family. His dad was on the City Council. His mom was a school teacher. He was going into his second year of college. I wasn't really worried about the case though, because none of the evidence was strong enough. The District Attorney tried to offer a plea deal. I told him what he could do with his plea deal, because we were taking this to trial.

Marcus and his parents were waiting for me outside the courtroom when I walked up.

"Hi Mr. and Mrs. King. I hugged Mrs. King. We had gotten close over the few months that I had taken her son Marcus' case.

"Your Honor I enter exhibit A, my client's cell phone records."

I also handed one to each one of the jurors.

"My client hadn't even spoken with the bank robber Ron until March 8th, which was the day the bank was robbed. He didn't have any time to plan this bank robbery. The only numbers on his cell phone bill are his parents' and his girlfriend's. Ron is an old high school friend. Marcus had just come home from school on a break. He stopped at his house and that is when Ron called him. All Marcus was told was that Ron wanted him to take him to the bank."

"I also enter exhibit B. This is the tape from the surveillance camera outside the bank. I put the disc inside the DVD player.

"Marcus took his time backing out of the parking lot. Ladies and gentlemen of the jury, if Marcus knew that Ron had just robbed the bank why is he taking his time pulling out the parking lot? The tape even showed Marcus wave to an elderly couple as they walked across the parking lot. I don't know about you but if I was part of a bank robbery I wouldn't be taking my time leaving the bank."

I was sitting in Showmars by the courthouse with Marcus and his parents waiting on the jury to deliberate. My phone went off, letting me know I had a text alert. I looked at the message. It was from Q.

Q: *Baby this ain't what u think. Please come home tonight so we can talk. Don't stay out tonight like u did last night.*

I laughed to myself. He was so dumb. I stayed in the house last night. He should have gotten his butt up and looked. My phone went off again. It was another text message from Q.

Q: *I know u probably in court right now and can't respond. Hit me when u get through.*

I never responded. I put my phone back in the case. It went off again. Q was starting to get on my nerves now. I grabbed the phone again, preparing to text him a piece of my mind. It wasn't Q this time. It was from a blocked number again.

Unknown: *Bitch I'm watching u.*

I looked around Showmars to see if anybody looked out of place. I didn't know who this was that kept talking about they were watching me.

A court clerk came over to our table and told me the jury had reached a verdict. We cleaned up our mess and headed back to the court house.

"We the jury finds the defendant Marcus King not guilty of all charges. Marcus grabbed me and hugged me tight.

"Thank you Neicee. He kissed me on my cheek. You are the best."

"You're welcome Marcus. It's my job. You a good kid. I never thought you had anything to do with the robbery. I just want you to finish school and make your parents proud. I'm gon' be checking up on you."

As I got to my car I noticed my tire was flat. I went around to survey it. Somebody had slashed my tire. I also noticed I had a note under my windshield wiper: *Bitch next time I'm gon' slash your face*. Enough was fucking enough. I didn't know who this was but I was getting ready to put my ear to the streets. I knew it had to be a bitch, because niggas didn't go through all this. I went to the trunk and grabbed my spare tire. I started to change my tire, but before I could get started I was interrupted.

"You look like you need some help with that tire." I looked up to see a sexy brother wearing the hell out of a Ralph Lauren suit. I started smiling.

"No, I don't need any help. I grew up with five brothers, so trust me, I know how to change a tire."

"Let me help you though. You too sexy to be changing a tire. I don't want you to break a nail." I started laughing. He reached his hand out to me to help me up. "My name is Terrance."

"My name is Shaneice."

When Terrance was through changing my tire he handed me his business card. I looked at the card and noticed he was also a lawyer. His card read Attorney Terrance Devaughn. I didn't tell him I was a lawyer too. I thanked him and got in my car. I rolled my window down to thank him again.

"I gave you my card for a reason Shaneice. I want you to use the number on the card. I would love to take you out sometime." I smiled and told him I would call. I drove off.

# *Chapter 9*

## Q

Damn this girl was crazy. I didn't know why she was still calling and sending me text messages. I had to figure out how to make things straight with Neicee and how to get this crazy bitch to leave me the fuck alone. I picked up the phone to call Neicee. She never picked up. I next called Tone.

"Yo what up nigga?" Tone said when he answered the phone. I told Tone everything that went down and how I might have to kill Leeka's ass. We kicked the breeze for a little bit. Tone also told me that D Dot drop was okay and we hung up the phone. I tried Neicee again and still no answer.

# Neicee

I pulled into the parking garage of my office building on Trade Street. I still had to meet with Mike and find out what last night was all about.

I walked past my secretary Shannon. I spoke to her and walked into my office. After about ten minutes of checking my email Shannon knocked on the door.

"Neicee." She called me Neicee because we were friends. I looked up at her.

"What's up girl?"

"First I want to ask you how was court? I know you won, because you are a beast in that courtroom."

"Girl you know I won. It was an open and shut case."

"Mike is here to see you and Q been calling all morning. I know he knows you was in court, but he kept asking if you came back to the office yet because he couldn't get you on the phone."

"Send Mike in. If Q calls back tell him I will call him back when I get through with my client.

When Mike walked in the office I offered him a seat.

"So do you want to tell me what the hell is going on Mike? I thought I told you to keep your nose clean. I don't know about this one. Why the hell did you kill a fucking cop?"

"Hold on Neicee. I ain't kill no cop. That's my word. I put that on my daughter. I ain't kill no cop. Detective Hill was a dirty cop. He had a partner named Officer Kirklen. Everybody called him Spooky. Spooky the one who killed Detective Hill. Detective Hill and Spooky had made a bust. Detective Hill kept most of the money and all the dope. I used to buy weight from both of them. I was with Detective Hill the day he got killed. He told me Spooky was looking for him. As I was pulling off Spooky was pulling up. He saw me. That's the one who probably gave the police the lead. Neicee you should see Spooky house. He living like he play for the Carolina Panthers. Don't no police make that much."

I listened as Mike spoke. Thoughts were running through my head. This was going to be a tough case. I would have to prove that it was some corrupt cops. If what Mike was telling me was true I knew we were in way too deep.

"Mike do you realize what you are telling me? This is some serious shit. We got cops killing cops and everything. I got you. I don't want you to worry about anything. Let me do the worrying because that's what you pay me for."

After my meeting with Mike I was through for today. I decided to head over to Tire Kingdom to get a new tire for my car. I called Q on the way.

"Hello," he answered on the first ring. I laughed to myself.

"Q I was just calling you back because I said I would. I'm headed to Tire Kingdom to get a new tire."

"Why you need a new tire? What's wrong with your tires? Your car ain't old enough to need new tires."

"Yeah I know. Somebody slashed my tire at the court house today."

"What do you mean somebody slashed your tire? Do you know who that somebody is?"

"Q if I knew who did it then I would be trying to do something about it. I don't know who did it. I guess it's the same person that's been sending me threatening messages. Whoever it is left me a note on my windshield. They also been calling my phone and sending me text messages."

"Neicee!" He yelled my name so loud I jumped. "Why the fuck is you just now telling me this bullshit? Somebody is threatening your ass and you ain't got shit to say? I'm putting one of my boys on you at all times until we figure out what the fuck is going on."

"I don't want any of your boys tailing me. I can handle myself. Why are you acting like you so concerned with me now? Get one of your boys to watch out for Leeka ass, because when I see her I'm gon' fuck her up. I don't give a damn about her being pregnant. While you at it get one of your boys to watch your back too." I hung up the phone on his dumb ass. I hated him.

I pulled into Tire Kingdom. When I pulled in all the men were rushing to my car to assist me.

"Hi, I'm Bruce," one of the employees said as he stuck his hand out to introduce himself. I had already seen his name on his uniform. I told Bruce what I needed and I walked into the customer's lounge. I went to the soda machine and got myself a ginger ale. I hadn't really been feeling good lately. My stomach was queasy. I sat down in a chair and checked my emails on my BlackBerry. It was a bunch of potential clients, some asking me about my fees, and some asking me for advice. I replied to the emails and put my phone back in the case.

Bruce walked up to me and told me my car was ready. "Somebody must really hate you." He made the comment while looking at my slashed tire.

"Yeah, I got some haters walking around here. I guess that means I'm doing something right." I grabbed my keys and got in my car.

# *Chapter 10*

## Q

I couldn't believe Neicee. I knew she was mad, but she should at least have let me protect her. It better not have been Leeka. I was gon' have to kill her for threatening Neicee. I was more pissed off at myself than anything. I had to always protect home. I didn't know why Leeka was even acting like this. I never made her think our relationship was more than it was. None of the other girls I messed with were tripping. I told them it was over and they were cool with it. I didn't really believe she was pregnant. Then again she might've been but the baby wasn't mine. I cheated, but I wasn't stupid. I didn't run up in any of them hos raw.

The only woman I went raw in was Neicee. Now if Neicee said she was pregnant then I would have believed her.

I had to get up out the bed. I couldn't keep lying in bed nursing my leg. I reached for my crutches. I got out the bed and went into the bathroom to wash up. I still couldn't get my leg wet. I went to the closet and grabbed my True Religion jeans and red True Religion shirt. I went back and sat in the room on the recliner we had in our room. I was going to wait on Neicee to come home.

An hour had passed before Neicee walked in the door. She ran over and sat in my lap and hugged me real tight. She caught me off guard, because I wasn't expecting that. I pulled back and gave her a deep tongue kiss. She didn't pull away. She kissed me with much force.

After the kiss she got off my lap and said we needed to talk. I explained to her that she didn't do nothing wrong. I was just being a man. I apologized for hurting her. I also told her I wasn't messing with Leeka anymore. She accepted my apology. Neicee also told me that it was going to be rough but she would try to put this behind us. She went on to tell me about what was going on with her. I promised her I wasn't going to let anything happen to her.

# Chapter 11

## Neicee

After my talk with Q I felt a little bit better. I still didn't trust him. No matter how good you be to a nigga they still find a way to cheat. I was not going to wait around on him to break my heart again. I was definitely getting ready to start getting out a little more. All of a sudden I felt dizzy. I needed to lay down for a few minutes. Q walked into the room to ask me if I wanted to ride out with him for a while, because he needed to get out the house. I told him to go ahead. I didn't want him to know I hadn't been feeling good.

"Neicee I ain't going to go chill with no broad. I want you to come with me, so you will know I ain't hiding nothing."

"Go ahead Q; you straight. I just don't want to go nowhere." To my surprise he took his clothes back off and got in the bed with me.

"If you don't want to go nowhere I ain't going nowhere either. I do need to make a few calls though and check on business."

After Q was through making his calls we laid in bed and watched Friday with Chris Tucker. That was one of my favorite movies. It always made me laugh.

When the movie went off I helped Q downstairs. He wanted to watch me cook. He said he enjoyed watching me cook so I decided to put on a show for him. I ran back upstairs and put on my short French maid uniform, and a pair of black Manolo pumps. The outfit showed off my legs. I went back downstairs and started to cook. I prepared a chicken casserole and some greens. I could feel Q burning a hole in the back of my ass.

I turned around and caught him staring.

"What?" He said.

"You trying to get something started, ain't you Neicee?" I just smiled and turned around to finish cooking. I loved these moments. As if on cue Q's phone rang. He didn't even try to hide it. He looked at me and said it was Leeka.

"Go ahead and answer it I told him." To my surprise he handed me the phone.

"Hello." I answered the phone. She didn't say anything though. She hung up. I looked at Q.

"She hung up the phone." He started laughing.

"Ha that bitch ain't that bad I see. Now that you answer the phone she ain't got nothing to say. I already told her don't make me turn you loose on her." We shared a laugh.

After dinner we went back upstairs. I went in the bathroom to take a shower. When I came out Q was on the phone arguing with someone. I assumed it was Leeka. He looked at me and motioned for me to come closer. I grabbed the phone from Q. I finished listening to her before I spoke. I heard her say she was gon' make sure I left Q.

"Leeka quit calling my man, okay? I am not going to leave Q. I would not give you the satisfaction. You keep yapping, talking about you pregnant by Q. I tell you what, I am gon' be a real woman about this. As long as you're pregnant don't bother us. We don't have anything to do with you being pregnant. When you have your baby then Q will get a DNA test. If the baby is his then he will do right by his seed. We ain't doing nothing for you right now. You are a ho. You wasn't anything but a jump off bitch."

"Oh is that what Q told you, that I was a jump off? You got me twisted Neicee. It is Q baby. He is gon' take care of me and my baby; you can believe that."

"Bitch get a life." I hung up the phone. Q was laughing.

"Neicee you a fool girl, you know that? I'm gon' change my number in the morning."

We made love the rest of the night. Inwardly I was crying but I never let a tear roll down my face. I didn't want Q to know how hurt I really was. I didn't want Q to know how hurt I really was. I put on a show for him and Leeka, but the pain of knowing that she might be pregnant by my man was more than I could bear. I put on such a great show I could have won an Academy Award.

The next morning I woke up in a hot sweat. I had to throw up. I ran to the bathroom. I didn't want Q to know something was wrong with me. I threw up in the toilet. I ran the water so Q wouldn't hear me. I washed my face and brushed my teeth and headed out the bathroom. I picked up my BlackBerry to check and see if I had any appointments today. I didn't have any, so I called Shannon and told her I would be working from home today. I told her to take messages and if anything was urgent to forward it to my BlackBerry.

A few hours later Q rolled over and looked at the clock.

"You ain't going to work today?"

"Nah. I'm gon' work from home today. All I really have to do is call Los, the private investigator that I work with sometimes." My phone went off with a text alert.

Unknown: *I c u didn't come to work today bitch.*

I looked at Q.

"What's wrong," he asked."

"Whoever the person is that is threatening me is really watching me. They just texted me and said they know I didn't go to work today."

"Do you have any idea who it could be?"

"No I don't. You know I don't really hang out that much."

# Q

Neicee might not have known who it was, but I had an idea. I bet it was Leeka. It couldn't be anyone else. When Neicee went to work tomorrow I'd have put a handle on this. In the meantime I needed to find out what was going on with Neicee. I noticed she hadn't been feeling too good. She'd been doing a good job at trying to hide it. I knew her though. I knew when something was wrong with her. I heard her in the bathroom running water.

I got up out the bed and walked to the bathroom. I opened up the door and saw her bent over the toilet puking her insides out.

"You okay?" She jumped when I asked her that, because I snuck up on her.

"Yeah, I'm okay." She got up and brushed her teeth and wiped her face.

She walked past me out the bathroom. I was looking at her the whole time.

"What?" she asked me.

"What's wrong with you Neicee? You don't think I noticed that something is wrong with you?"

"I said it's nothing Q, damn. Leave me alone." I followed right behind her.

# Neicee

Q was starting to get on my damn nerves. Why was he so concerned about me? I knew what's wrong with me. I was pregnant. I had always wanted to have his baby, but not now. I wanted to give him his first born. I wanted us to share that together. With Leeka saying she was pregnant the sight of Q made me sick. I didn't really know how much longer I was planning on being in this relationship. If the baby was his I knew I couldn't continue this relationship. I couldn't look at the baby every day knowing that Q cheated on me to get this baby. I needed to make me a doctor's appointment first thing tomorrow. I got up and went into the study to get on Facebook.

I logged into my Facebook account. I had another message from Dark Sexy. I sent him a message. I saw that he was online. I asked him what his real name was, and I gave him mine. He sent me his phone number. I sent him a message back: *Okay Ron, I will call you.* I logged off of Facebook and picked up my phone to call Los, a private investigator who I worked with sometimes. I explained to him what Mike told me. He told me he was on it and we disconnected the call.

When I walked back into the room, Q was watching Bad Boys with Will Smith and Martin Lawrence. I laid across the bed to watch it with him. I loved me some Will Smith. When the commercial came on Q was staring at me.

"What?" I asked.

"You know what. What's going on with you? Why you so sick lately?"

"It ain't nothing I can't handle Q.

"Neicee, talk to me. Don't act like that. I thought we was better than that. Why you keeping secrets and shit?"

"I ain't keeping no secrets. I don't really know what's wrong with me. I got an idea, but I don't know. I think I might be pregnant, but that would be a tragedy."

Q had a hurt look on his face. He was quiet for a minute before he spoke.

"Why would that be tragedy Neicee? You don't want a baby with me?"

"No…yes…I don't know," I said as tears started rolling down my face. "I don't even know if I still want to be with you. If I could rewind time this would be one of the happiest moments in my life. I wanted to share bringing our first child into this world with you. I don't want to share my pregnancy with no one. Even if Leeka's baby ain't yours I got to go through my whole pregnancy with her."

"Is that what you think Neicee? I am sorry I hurt you. Knowing that I hurt you hurts me even more. If you walked out my life I would be empty. Please don't kill my baby. Leeka's baby ain't mine. I did sleep with her, but she get around. That baby ain't mine. You're not going to go through this pregnancy alone. You know I'm gon' be here for you."

I looked at Q. He turned his face away from mine. I knew he didn't want me to see him cry. I had never seen him cry. He always tried to play the tough guy role with me.

"I don't know Q. I have been faithful to you the whole relationship. You don't hear my name in the streets. When you met me couldn't any of your boys say they had been with me. I feel betrayed in the worst way. You're making me look like a fool."

"Fuck them hos. I don't give a damn what they got to say. Those hos just jealous of you anyway." He got up and threw the remote on the bed.

I heard him trying to get down the steps with his crutches. I also heard when the garage door opened and he pulled out. I reached for the phone and called my mom. I hadn't talked to my mom in a few days. I needed to hear her voice. I also admired my mom. She raised six kids by herself. My dad walked out on her when I was four years old and my oldest brother Lamont stepped up to be the man of the house. He was 15 years old at the time. I always looked up to him for that. Since I was the only girl I had it real rough, but it only made me stronger. I had a close family.

My mom picked up the phone. "Hello."

"Hey Mom," I said.

"Hey baby. I ain't heard from you in a while. I just told your brother Jason I was going to file a missing persons report, because I hadn't heard from you."

Jason was the youngest boy. He was two years older than me.

"Ma you could've called me. I don't have to be the one who calls all the time."

"Yes, you do. It's only one of me. I got six people to call every day when y'all only got one," she said jokingly. "What's wrong with you though? You sound sad."

"I'm okay Ma. My mom always knew when something was wrong with me, but I knew she wouldn't pry. She knew I would tell her when I was ready. One thing about my mom was that she never got in her kids' business. She always had our back. I don't know about Tyler Perry's Madea but I knew I had a live one. My mom was sweet as long as you didn't break her number one rule. Everybody knew not to mess with Denise's kids.

"Okay Neicee. I'm here if you need to talk."

I hated lying to my mom but I didn't like my family all in my business. I would make up with Q, and they would still be mad at him. I wasn't going to be one of those women that wondered why their family didn't like their man.

We hung up. I went to the bathroom to take a shower. When I got out the shower I had another text message.

Unknown: *I know you still trying to figure out who I am. Just know that I'm watching you.*

I decided I wasn't going to let that bother me. I fell asleep.

# *Chapter 12*

## Q

*A week later.*

Neicee left the house today. She said she had some early appointments. I knew she didn't, because I had already checked her BlackBerry. A nigga was getting paranoid. I cheated on her and I didn't trust her. She was starting to act real sneaky lately. We never talked anymore about her being pregnant. I had been keeping a close watch on her at home though. My leg was getting better, so I could get around a little more. I picked up the phone to call her.

"Hello," she said when he picked up the phone. I could hear background noise, so I knew she wasn't at the office.

"Where you at?'

"I'm meeting with a client. Why?"

"Let me take you to lunch when you leave your client."

"Q I got a long day. I will see you when I get home." She hung up the phone.

I couldn't believe this girl just hung up the phone on me like that. I put some clothes on and left out the door. I decided to check on some of my spots on the West Side. I decided I would roll up on these niggas. I had to make sure nobody was trying to cheat me out of none of my money. I also had to get with

Tone so I could catch up with that nigga Ron. His days

were numbered.

I dialed Tone's number. He picked up the

phone.

"What up Q? I was just getting ready to hit you.

We need to handle this Ron situation. Meet me at the

Wendy's on Sugar Creek."

I pulled up in Wendy's parking lot. Tone was

sitting in his whip. Tone was into those old classic cars.

He had a 1988 Caprice Classic sitting on 26s. He also

had a 2014 silver CL Class Sport Mercedes. It was fully

loaded with a CD player, MP3 player, and satellite

radio. He only drove that car on the weekend.

When I got out the car a group of girls walked by. They were checking out my ride. I had a black 2015 BMW 745 Series with cream leather seats and the wood grain. It was fully loaded also with some 24s. I waved to the ladies and walked over and gave Tone some dap.

"You got here quick as hell my nigga," Tone said.

"I was already out. I'm gon' dead this nigga tonight. He ain't gon' even feel me coming. I got my twins with me." Tone fell out laughing, because he knew I was talking about my nines. I called them my twins. I carried one on each side.

After Tone and I grabbed some food we headed over to West Boulevard. I had a few apartments in the projects called Little Rock. I had a few chicken heads

that let me set up shop in their cribs. All I had to do was

throw them about $500 a month. They were set,

because their rent wasn't but about $20 a month. They

were really stupid though, because they should've been

charging me more than that. I didn't touch any dope.

Tone didn't either. We let the young boys handle that. I

had a few look out boys. They were anywhere from 15

to 18 years old. They let us know what was going on in

the hood. I paid them about $300 a day. My street

soldiers I paid a G a day. I had to keep them happy

though. They were some real thorough dudes; three of

the hardest niggas around. They had a huge body count.

They wouldn't hesitate to put a bullet in you. They

wasn't with me at the club that night. If they were Ron

would've got deaded that night. They didn't miss their

mark. I also had a few lieutenants. They ran their own spots. They had boys up under them. I was a decent dude as long as you didn't cross me when it came to my money.

I pulled beside Tone in the parking lot of Little Rock Apartments. We both got out the car and headed upstairs to Michelle crib. She stayed on the top floor. I turned the doorknob and it was locked. I knew something wasn't right. Michelle knew better than to lock the door. Since the door was locked I knew something was wrong. That was the code we set up to warn me.

Tone noticed too, because I saw him pull out his Glock. We both noticed Craig, the neighborhood crack head. Tone walked over to him and told him he would bless him if he knocked on Michelle's door like he wanted to buy something.

Craig knocked on Michelle's door while me and Tone waited on the side with our guns drawn. I heard Michelle ask him who it was and what he wanted.

"Michelle open the door. I got money this time."

I also heard someone inside tell Michelle to open the door. When she opened the door Tone snatched her out, and we ran in firing. Them niggas wasn't even prepared. I shot the first nigga in the middle of his forehead. I was firing with both my nines. By this time they were firing back. I ducked behind the couch. I saw Tone throw the table in front of him and he popped back up and shot the nigga in his eye. The nigga wasn't even dead. I fired one straight to his dome.

I heard the sirens outside. I looked at Tone. I knew we had to leave. I wasn't worried about anything. Michelle knew how to handle the police. We casually walked out the apartment and blended in with the crowd. The police ran right past us. I ducked in Lisa's spot. Tone followed right behind me. She was a crack head. I gave her $50 and told her to shut up. She agreed with fear in her eyes. Slowly she became anxious. I guess she realized she could cop some dope.

"Lisa, why don't you do something positive with your money? It's June, and it's hot. Buy your boys some ice cream or something."

She nodded and walked off to her bedroom. I knew what I said went in one ear and out the other. She didn't care about nothing I said. I hated that I even gave her that. I didn't have time for her though. I needed to change my clothes so I could get out the hood. In the heat of everything I don't know how the police missed the blood on our clothes. I was grateful but I didn't want to chance it.

Tone walked up to me.

"I called Na Na; she on the way with some clothes for us. I told her to be here like yesterday."

Na Na walked in the door with a shopping bag. I guess she wanted the boys in blue to think she stayed there and had been out shopping. One thing I could say about me and Tone is we had some down broads. Na Na was looking good as hell. She had her hair done up in a mohawk. She had on a pink Fetish mini dress. Fetish was written in black across the front. It was off the shoulder. You could see her sexy tattoo. Her and Neicee had matching tattoos. She had on a pair of black peep toe platform sandals by House of Dereon. She also had on gold and pink bracelets with pink earrings. Just like Neicee all she wore was Mac lip gloss. They wouldn't wear any makeup. Na Na was a doctor. She only worked part time now though ever since her and Tone had Ashanti. She was a big time surgeon. We had to use her from time to time to keep the police out our business.

Tone grabbed the bag out her hand.

"Thank you babe," he said as he kissed her on the cheek. She pushed him off of her.

"Don't be touching me with all that blood on you. Y'all need to go change so we can bounce. You ain't got time for no shower. Just get the bloody clothes off."

I changed in the bathroom. Tone must have changed in the living room, because I heard Na Na ask Lisa what the fuck she was looking at. I also heard Lisa say this was her damn house.

I walked out just in time, because Tone was holding Na Na.

"Come on y'all." That was Na Na talking to me and Tone.

"I'm gon' take y'all to my sister Jazmine house over in Wilmore. Just leave your cars. I will bring y'all back over here later."

When we got in the car my Nextel went off. It was one of my boys, Rick from the block. I responded and told him to hit me on my iPhone. I didn't want to talk on the Nextel just in case the cops picked it up on their radio wave.

I answered the iPhone.

"What's up Rick?"

"I just wanted to let you know that those was Ron boys. You need to take care of that nigga. He acting stupid since he shot you and you ain't do nothing about it."

"Thank you Rick, but that nigga gon' get it. I already had plans for his ass. I updated Tone on what Rick said. We both agreed we would discuss our plans at Na Na's sister Jazmine's house.

# Chapter 13

## Neicee

I had just hung up the phone with Q when Ron walked back to the table. I finally called him. Today was our first time meeting. I met him in the food court in Concord Mills Mall. His pictures did him no justice. He was rocking a green Sean Jean shirt and a pair of Sean Jean jeans. The Nike Airmaxes on his feet were green and white also. He was dark-skinned with the prettiest white teeth, and hazel eyes. His cornrows looked like he had just got out the chair. I was rocking a Michael Kors blue jean dress, and a pair of open toe metallic sandals with the zipper opening on the heel. They were real cute. They were also Michael Kors. To top it off I had my cute little mirror box Michael Kors

clutch bag.

He handed me my food. I was having a hard

time keeping food down. I still hadn't made it to the

doctor's office yet. I would stop by Walgreens when I

left and get me a home pregnancy test.

"Thank you," I said.

"Oh you welcome shorty." He had ordered us

some pizza from Sabarro's.

"I'm glad you finally decided to call a nigga.

I've been talking to you for a minute on Facebook. You

are prettier in person though."

I was smiling on the inside. He was real cool to be around. I knew it couldn't really be anything though. I knew he knew who Q was because he was in the game. Q was a major player in Charlotte. He pushed heavy weight. I didn't want there to be any blood spilled. I knew Q would kill this nigga if he caught me with him. I'd had my fun.

I talked to Ron for a little longer and he asked me if I wanted to go shopping. I looked at him like he was crazy.

"What kind of question is that?" I jokingly asked him.

"We in a mall. You know I want to shop."

I hoped he didn't think he was getting no ass. He dropped $2,000 on me, but that was nothing. I had my own money. Plus Q always spent more than that on me when we went shopping. After we walked out the Nike outlet I told him I needed to get home. I told him I would call him later even though I knew I probably wouldn't.

He walked me to my car. When we got to my car I gave him a hug and got in.

"Don't be no stranger," he said to me.

"I won't." I drove off. I put in the Ashanti CD. I had to hear my song. I was singing along to the lyrics of "I Got That Good Good" when my cell phone went off. I turned off the radio. It was my work phone and it was a blocked number so I assumed one of my clients was locked up.

"Hello," I said.

"This is a prepaid call. You will not be charged for this call. This call is from a federal prisoner. Peanut."

I pressed five. He took so long to call I had forgot I gave him my number.

"Hey Ne Ne. What the business is?"

"Hey Peanut. You took so long to call me I forgot I gave you my number. Why are you just now calling me? It's been almost two weeks. It don't take that long to get my number on your list."

"I just wanted to give you some space Ne Ne. I know a nigga just kind of reappeared on you. I don't

know what you got going on in your life and I can't
invade your space like that."

I must have been too quiet, because I heard
Peanut ask me if I was still on the phone.

"Yes, I am here. I just got a lot on my mind."

"Well Ne Ne you know you can tell me. We
have always been friends. I know when something is
bothering you."

For the rest of the time I found myself confiding
in Peanut about everything. I told him how I thought I
was pregnant and was headed to get a pregnancy test
from Walgreens as we spoke. I also told him about Q
cheating on me and about Leeka being pregnant. I also
told him how I was just tired and was thinking about

moving to Atlanta, Georgia. He was the only person I had told that to. I had always wanted to stay there, but my life was in Charlotte. The 15 minutes was up before I realized it. Peanut promised he would call me back later to find out the results of my pregnancy test.

As I was driving down 85 South I thought a lot about my situation. I was seriously thinking about moving to Atlanta. I had a friend there that I went to law school with. She was thinking about starting her own firm and wanted me to help her since I already had my own firm here. I kept telling her no, but with everything that was going on I felt like I needed to start over. I also thought about Peanut. He hung out in the streets a lot, but I didn't ever feel like he was cheating on me. I never heard another female talk about how they had my man. I knew he loved me with all his heart but he loved the streets too.

I pulled into the parking lot of Walgreens on the corner of W. T. Harris and North Tryon. I went into the store and got me an EPT and a bag of cheese Bugles. I got back into my car and headed home. I didn't turn the radio on because I needed to clear my head.

I was standing in the bathroom anxiously awaiting the results of my pregnancy test. It came back positive just like I knew it would. I left the pregnancy test there so Q would see it. I didn't want to talk to him so I would just let him find out on his own. I knew I had to make a doctor's appointment first thing in the morning. My house phone rang. I grabbed the cordless phone and looked at the caller ID. It was Na Na.

"Hello," I said. "Why are you calling my house phone and not my cell phone?"

"I tried calling your cell phone. You didn't pick up, but anyway that ain't the reason why I am calling. Some stuff has jumped off and I'm on my way over to talk to you about it."

I said okay and I hung up. I went downstairs to wait on Na Na to get here. While I was waiting I went into the kitchen to get a glass of orange juice. I love orange juice. When I was putting my glass in the sink I heard the doorbell ring. I opened the door for Na Na.

"Hi," she said as she shut the door behind her. She followed me to the couch in the living room. She told me about what happened with Q and Tone. I knew a war had just begun in the streets. Q felt like he had something to prove. I also told her about me being

pregnant.

"Na Na I can't go through this right now with Q. I love him, but I got a baby on the way. It ain't all about me and him no more. I am hurt to the core right now because of Leeka talking about she is pregnant." I started crying.

Na Na hugged me tight. We had been friends since kindergarten. She felt all my pain. "Let it out Neicee. I know you hurt."

"Why would he do this to me Na Na? What is wrong with me? I have been nothing but good to him. I have never cheated on him. I have niggas coming on to me all the time. Do you know how many niggas would love to take his spot?"

"No Neicee there ain't nothing wrong with you. Don't let that nigga make you second guess yourself. You are well kept. Next to me you are the flyest diva I know."

I started laughing because she said next to her.

"You are a trip Na Na. You always know how to make me smile." I started telling her about Peanut and how he was getting ready to get out. Just talking about Peanut put a smile on my face. Peanut always made me happy.

"Well Neicee you know I stand behind whatever decision you make. I know you love Q and if you really want it to work at least wait until Leeka has the baby. Personally I don't think the baby is his. That girl is a straight up dirty butt. I know it's going to be hard. I love you girl. You are like a sister to me."

I hugged Na Na and watched her get in her car and drive off. She was driving her fire red 2011 Infiniti G37. It had the built-in six-disc CD changer and MP3 player just like mine. Tone surprised her with her car around the same time Q surprised me with mine. Her car was four doors though, because of her daughter Ashanti.

I went upstairs and took a shower. I then got in the bed. I was tired.

# Chapter 14

## Q

I was laying low in a van that me and Tone rented from a crack head. We were sitting in the parking lot of a hotel off of Sugar Creek Road. We were waiting on Ron. We had gotten a tip from a broad I knew. She said Ron was meeting her there. We noticed a black Chevy Impala pull in the parking lot. I knew it was Ron so I cocked my gun. As I was cocking my gun a police car rolled through. I knew they were patrolling the area. I also knew that I would have to get Ron another day. I pulled out the parking lot.

I went back to my car. I told Tone to drop the car back off. I was going home to check on Neicee. I picked up the phone to call her but I got her voicemail.

I tried it again and again I got the voicemail. I gave up and took the car on to the house. I was hoping she would be there when I got there.

Neicee's car was in the garage when I pulled in. That made me feel a little better. I knew she was safe. She was laying in the bed looking so peaceful when I came in the room. I went over and kissed her on the forehead. I knew how that drove her crazy. I headed to the bathroom to take a shower.

When I got out the shower I noticed her pregnancy test sitting on the sink. I saw the pink and I was happy as hell. My baby was pregnant. I walked into the bedroom with the test in my hand. I went over and gave her the wettest kiss.

"You having my baby?" I asked her.

"That's what the results say Q."

I held Neicee all night long. I was too happy about her being pregnant. I knew then I had to change my lifestyle. I couldn't bring a baby into this world with my lifestyle. I had to make her my wife. I was going to do right by her and my baby. She didn't know how much this meant to me.

# Neicee

I awoke the next morning to the smell of bacon. I looked at the clock. It read 8:30. I went to the bathroom to wash up and brush my teeth. When I got downstairs Q was cooking. He looked up at me and smiled. "Hey mom," he said to me. I just smiled back at him. "Have a seat. Breakfast is almost done. I made pancakes, bacon, and fresh fruit. I sat down and waited on him to finish.

Over breakfast we made small talk. I was still not feeling Q. I was happy about my baby, but I wasn't happy about the timeframe. All I could think about was sharing my pregnancy with Leeka. Q must have sensed that something was wrong because when I looked up he was staring at me.

"What's wrong Neicee?"

"I just got a lot on my mind Q. I'm happy about my pregnancy, but I just can't get over sharing it with Leeka."

"Neicee I promise you I'm going to be there every step of the way. I'm not going to miss a doctor's appointment. That's my word."

I got up from the table. I told Q I had to go to work. I was only doing half a day. I promised him I would make a doctor's appointment.

When I got to work I told Shannon to make me a OB/GYN appointment . She looked at me and screamed.

"Oh my God Neicee. I'm so happy for you."

I went in my office. As I was sitting at my desk Shannon called out to me saying Los, my private investigator, was on line one.

"Hello," I said as I picked up the phone. Los went on to explain to me that I was indeed working with some crooked cops. I knew I was in way over my head, but I was a big girl I could handle it. I hung up with Los I called Mike. I told him to meet me in my office on Monday at three so we could discuss his case. We hung up. Shannon stuck her head in my door and told me my doctor's appointment was on Monday at 9:15.

I called Q to let him know about my doctor's appointment on Monday. I heard my cell phone alert me of a text message.

Unknown: *I c u made it to work today. I got my eye on u.*

I was seriously thinking about changing my number. This was a crazy person I'm dealing with. I grabbed my things to go home. I sent Ron a quick text message before I left out the door. He responded back before I got to my car. I decided to call him since I was about to drive.

Ron picked up the phone on the second ring.

"What's up ma? he asked me when he picked up the phone. "A nigga is glad to hear from you. What your sexy ass been up to? Meet me somewhere so I can buy you some lunch."

I was grinning from ear to ear. Normally Q was the only nigga that could put a smile on my face like that. Lately all he had brought me was tears. I was tired of crying.

"Where you at now?" I asked him.

"I'm on the North Side in North Charlotte." We agreed to meet at Wild Wings at the Epic Center and we hung up.

I agreed to meet him at the Epic Center because I knew Q's boys didn't frequent there so it was safe. To my surprise Ron was already there when I walked in the door. *A punctual man. I like that.* I gave him a hug and took my seat.

"I'm surprised you beat me here," I said to Ron.

"Did you think I would leave your sexy ass sitting here by yourself for another nigga to snatch you up? I gotta have you for real." He had me smiling but I knew truthfully we couldn't be together. Q would kill both of us and I knew it. I knew I was playing with fire. Now that I knew I'm pregnant I was going to have to stop talking to him.

After my lunch date with Ron I decided to head home. I was hoping Q wasn't at home because I didn't feel like being bothered with him. I knew something was happening to our relationship and I didn't like it. Q was my heart and I always enjoyed spending time with him but ever since that Leeka mess something just happened. I knew I needed to talk to him about it. I couldn't fix my relationship with him by creeping with someone else. I wasn't even that kind of person and I didn't want anybody taking me out of my element. My birthday was coming up June 12th and I didn't know what I wanted to do. It was in three weeks.

Q was outside in the pool when I got home. I decided to join him. I went to the pool room and put on my swimsuit. I sat on the edge of the pool and put my feet in because I didn't want to get my hair wet. Q came over and pulled me in the pool.

"Q don't get my hair wet," I said jokingly. That made it worse because he started splashing water on me. I was laughing. He dunked my whole head in the water.

""t's on now," I said to him. I dove under the water and pulled him under by his legs. We were play fighting under the water. When we came up he pulled me towards him and kissed me. To my surprise I enjoyed the kiss.

Q helped me out the water and led me to our Jacuzzi . He pulled his swimming trunks off before he got in. I followed him and took off my swimming suit as well.

"Sit on the step baby," he instructed me. I did as I was told. He pushed my legs apart and dove head first into my pussy. He spread my pussy lips apart with his mouth and stuck his tongue in my hole. I was about to go crazy. The sound of him eating me out had me losing my mind. I grabbed his head because it felt so good. I had multiple orgasms. After he was done he started teasing me by rubbing the head of his dick over my pussy. He knew that drove me crazy. He put my left titty in his mouth and begin to suck on it like he was a baby and this was his last meal. By this time he had stuck his dick in my pussy and was slow grinding me. It was feeling so good. I was biting down on my lip.

"Baby I'm so sorry," he whispered in my ear. I silenced him with a kiss on his lips. I kissed him with everything in me.

We ended up making love all over the house. We were exhausted and hungry. We decided to order some Chinese food.

# Chapter 15

## Q

Neicee was in the shower when I heard her text message alert. I thought it was from whoever had been threatening her so I looked at it. It was from somebody she had under the name R. No name; just R. My antenna went up. The text message read.

R: *I enjoyed u today. Lunch was fun with ur sexy ass. We must do this again.*

I was heated. I was going to kill this nigga. I waited on Neicee's ass to get out the shower. I was ending this shit today. When she walked into the bedroom I wasted no time.

"Did you fuck him?"

"What are you talking about Q?" I had tears in my eyes by now. I could not take another man fucking my woman. I put her phone in her face and asked her again.

"Did you fuck him?" She put her head down. I saw the tears falling from her face. I took that as a yes. I threw the phone against the wall, but it didn't break. The case fell apart though. I knew I had done some shit but this shit really hurt and I couldn't fathom this.

"I didn't fuck him Q," I faintly heard her say. "I didn't fuck him. I went out with him a few times because I was hurting and I wanted to hurt you back but I didn't fuck him. You know me Q. You know I don't sleep around." I looked her in her face.

"No, I thought I knew you." I put on some sweats and left the house.

I was hurting real bad and I didn't know how to deal with it. I believed Neicee when she said she didn't sleep with him, but knowing she thought about it was bothering me. I knew I had done some dirty stuff but she was not supposed to do that. I was not really mad at her; I was mad at myself. I shouldn't have even gave her room to think about another nigga. I remember when her smile was so bright it would light up the whole room. I didn't even see my baby smile any more. I had to fix this. I got on the phone with Neicee's legal secretary Shannon. I wanted to find out her schedule for the week. I was taking her on a vacation. Shannon told me Neicee was free for the rest of the week next week after Tuesday. My next call was to my travel agent. We decided on a trip to Vegas.

My next call was to my jeweler. I told her to pick me out five of her best engagement rings and I would be there to take a look at them. I hung up with her and continued to drive and think. I was ready to settle down. I had a baby on the way and Neicee was a good woman. I was tired of messing around on her. After driving around for two hours I headed home.

Neicee was laying in the bed with the TV on but no volume. She was playing Kelly Price's "Tired." She looked up at me, but she didn't say a word. I didn't say anything either. I went and got in the shower.

When I got out the shower the TV was off. I slipped in the bed behind Neicee and I grabbed her to cuddle. I whispered in her ear.

"I love you." We fell asleep just like that.

I woke up the next morning because I heard Neicee in the bathroom throwing up. I got up to check on her. She was standing over the toilet. I held her hair for her. When she was done she brushed her teeth and laid back in the bed. I told her I was going to get her some crackers from the kitchen. When I walked back into the room I looked at her and told her we need to talk.

"Q this is not what you think. I didn't sleep with Ron. I wouldn't do that to you."

"Wait a minute Neicee. Who is Ron?"

"Ron is R. That's the man who sent the text messages."

"What does Ron look like?"

I couldn't believe who Neicee was explaining to me.

"Neicee that's the nigga that shot me."

"Oh my God Q. Are you serious? I wonder if he knew I was your girl."

"He don't know. If he knew he would have tried to kill you and he didn't. I want you to bring that nigga to me."

I went over my plan with Neicee. My plan was for Neicee to meet with him and I was going to kill that nigga. The next day was Saturday and that's when it was going down. Neicee and I hung out the rest of the day. We went to Babies 'R' Us to look at baby furniture. Neicee kept looking at this rocking chair. I could tell she wanted it but she wouldn't say it. I made a mental note about it. I was going to hand the sales lady my card and slip her some cash. I made a mental note of everything she was looking at. It was a lot of stuff so I knew it was hard to decide. Next we hit Baby Gap. She went crazy in that store. She bought all neutral colors like green and yellow. We didn't know the sex of the baby, but she wanted to buy and I had no problem with that. After hitting all the high end baby stores we stopped at Angie's Diner on Beatties Ford Road. It was a soul food restaurant, so I ordered turkey wings with mac and cheese and some cabbage. Neicee ordered some fish with cabbage and candied yams. We got our food and headed home.

When we got home Neicee shot Ron a text message asking him to meet her at the Epic Center the next day. They decided on a movie. The movie theater at the Epic Center served full meals. I knew I was going to go crazy while they were on their date. The plan was after they left the date I was going to be waiting on Ron in the parking lot in his car. We took a shower together and fell asleep.

The next morning I woke up and I told Neicee I had a few errands to run before our plans later on this evening. She said okay and went back to sleep. I had to go see my jeweler. I was going to propose to her in Vegas.

I left out of my jeweler's with a three-carat princess cut diamond ring. It was 14-carat white gold. It cost me almost $6,000. I knew my baby was going to like the ring. There was no doubt in my mind. I stopped by the travel agent and picked up our tickets and headed on home.

When I walked in the house Neicee was on the phone. She threw her hand up indicating for me to be quiet. I knew she was on the phone with Ron. It messed my head up to hear her call him baby, but I knew she was playing a role. She ended the call.

# Neicee

I sat across from Ron making small talk. Knowing this nigga tried to kill my baby just pissed me off. I had nothing for him. He kept grabbing my hand. His touch just disgusted me.

"So Neicee when are you going to be my woman? I need you on my team."

"Well I guess we will see Ron," I said with a fake smile on my face. I was thinking to myself that this nigga couldn't even smell my pussy. My phone was on vibrate, but I felt it going off. I knew it was Q. I didn't want to give Ron any suspicions. Ron excused himself to the rest room.

While Ron was in the restroom I took the time to check my phone. I texted Q back and told him I would send him a message when we were leaving the building. I placed my phone back in my purse just as Ron approached the table.

"Let's get out of here," he said to me. He pulled my chair out and helped me out the seat. I never texted Q back. If the situation was different I could have given Ron a chance. He was a gentleman. I met Q first, and he tried to kill him, so the idea was forgotten as soon as it was thought about.

As we were walking to the car Ron pulled a fast one on me.

"Bitch did you think I didn't know who the fuck you was?" he said this as he had his hands around my neck. He was choking me. In a way I was regretting not calling Q. Ron pushed me up against a nearby BMW. I was praying the alarm went off, but it didn't.

"It took me a minute to realize who the fuck you was bitch. Leeka sent me a text message while we were eating asking me why was I out with Q girlfriend."

I held my hands up trying to pry his hands from around my neck.

I heard Ron talking, but I didn't know what he was saying. I was trying to reach for my nine millimeter that I had tucked in the back of my pants. Q didn't know that I was planning on killing this nigga myself. That's why I never sent him a text message. Ron pushed me into another car. That was my chance.

He had just made the biggest mistake that was going to cost him his life. When I hit the car I reached in the back of my pants and pulled out my gun. I cocked it and put a bullet straight in his dome. My gun had a silencer on it so no one even heard him. I stepped over him in my black Manolo Blahnik pumps. I thought I would feel a certain way after catching my first body. I did not. He was going to kill me; I had to tell myself that. I did what I had to do.

When I looked up Q jumped out the car and grabbed me. He placed me in his car and sped to the security booth. He pointed his gun at the guard and demanded the video surveillance. He then made the guard give him his driver's license. No words were spoken between me and Q as we pulled out the parking garage.

The first thing I did when I walked in the house was take a shower. Q had long gone to get rid of the gun for me. He should've been returning soon. Before I could lay down good I heard the alarm announcing the garage door was open. Q asked me if I was okay when he walked into the room. I looked at him and told him yes. I knew this would never be spoken of again.

# Chapter 15

## Neicee

We weren't even halfway into the movie before Q started messing with me. He was massaging my titties through my shirt. He then lifted my shirt up over my head. I had on a yellow cami and a pair of yellow boy shorts. Yellow was Q's favorite color so I already knew the color alone turned him on. He put one titty in his mouth as he kept massaging the other one. He knew how to get me aroused. I loved for my titties to be sucked. I watched him as he flicked his tongue across my titty. He then stuck his hand down my panties and rubbed my clit. He stuck one finger in and then two. I could feel my juices running. He then stuck his finger in his mouth.

"Damn Neicee," he whispered into my ear. I could hear his tongue lashing on my juices as he was eating me out. I was about to explode. I begged him to put it in. He wanted to tease me.

"Let me ride Q."

Q laid down as I asked him to. I got on top and rode him like my life depended on it. "You wanted it, you better get it. You better not stop either." I rode even harder while Q was whispering those words to me. It felt so good. My eyes were rolling. I was on the brink of an orgasm. Q flipped me over and pushed both of my legs above my head.

"Give it to me Q. Oh baby please give it to me." I heard my juices when I exploded. It went pop and ran all down my thighs. Q kept right on going. When he finally came he exploded all on my titties. We both just laid there for a while. We were exhausted.

Q got up first and he ran us some bath water. He put some Epsom salt in the water. He knew I was sore. Q helped me into the tub and he climbed in right behind me. I leaned my head against his chest as he ran his fingers through my hair. He whispered in my ear that we were going to be alright. He also told me about the upcoming trip he had planned for us. I wished Tone and Na Na could come with us, but we both agreed we needed that alone time. I was excited about the trip. I couldn't wait to go shopping. I knew I would be getting big soon but oh well. Monday I had a doctor's appointment to find out how far along I was.

After our bath I fell asleep in Q's arms. I awakened to turkey bacon, grits, toast, and fresh fruit. I turned my phone back on while Q was hand feeding me some grapes. I had 20 text messages. Nineteen of them were from my stalker. One of them was from Na Na telling me to call her when I was free. I dialed her number. She answered on the first ring.

"What's up chick?" she said to me. We chitchatted some more. I told her about my doctor's appointment on Monday. She said she wanted to go with me but Q asked her if he can have this one for himself and she agreed.

The next morning was Sunday. I decided to go to church. I hadn't been to church in a while. I woke Q up to tell him to get ready for church. I was going back to my roots. Free Will Ministries on Beatties Ford Road was my church. I hadn't been there in years. I knew better than that. I knew my Grandma was probably turning over in her grave. She raised us in the church. My mom barely went herself. I knew Pastor Sallie Lauderdale was going to be happy to see me.

Just as I expected when I walked in the church her whole face lit up. I walked in during praise service. She asked me if I wanted to testify. I agreed and stood up to tell the whole church I was expecting and how God had brought me through a lot.

After church I stayed behind to talk to Pastor Lauderdale. She told me how happy she was to see me and not to stay gone away so long. She told me she was praying for us and not to forget that Jesus always carried me in the midst of all my storms. Those words meant so much to me. I don't think she knew how much she had touched my heart with those words.

After we left the church Q drove us to Dave and Busters in Concord Mills Mall. He knows how much I liked to bowl and play video games. Both of us were kids at heart.

We bowled a few games, ate some wings, and headed on home. On the ride home we talked about a lot of things. We also talked about baby names. Of course if it was a boy he wanted a junior. I told him that was fine. If it was a girl we were going to name her Quintina Shanese. We were both excited about the doctor's appointment tomorrow and the fact that we were going on vacation Tuesday. We really needed this time together.

The next morning Q drove us to my doctor's appointment. He held my hand the whole wait.

"Shaneice Love," I heard the nurse say. We jumped up and followed her. She took us to a scale first.

"I need to see how much you weigh Ms. Love." I stepped on the scale. It said I weighed one hundred and thirty five pounds. I had put on some weight. Next she told me that Dr. Breamer wanted me to do an ultrasound.

I looked over at Q as we listened to the baby heartbeat. I could see a single tear roll down his cheek. I was further along than I thought. The lady said I was 17 weeks and asked if we wanted to know the sex of the baby. We both shook our heads yes. She then hit us with something we were not expecting. She said we were expecting twins; she heard two heartbeats. That alone made me cry. "Congratulations! You're having a boy and a girl," she said. Q stood up and gave me a wet kiss on my lips.

"Baby you just made me the happiest man alive."

Dr. Breamer walked in after the ultrasound tech left. "Congratulations are in order," she said as she looked at us. I looked at her and smiled. She wrote me a prescription for some prenatal vitamins and set me an appointment for the following week.

Q and I were on cloud nine when we left the doctor's office. We decided to keep it a secret until we got back from our trip. On the way home we talked about whether we should do separate nurseries or just one for the first year. We didn't have as much time as we thought we had. We decided to just wait until we got back from our trip.

I packed both of our bags when we got to the house. I was so excited about our trip. I took a long hot shower and laid in the bed. Q had stepped out for a few hours. He had to handle some business before we left in the morning.

I had dozed off. I was awakened by a notification on my cell phone alerting me that I had a text message. I looked at it and realized it was my stalker. This was really starting to piss me off because I didn't have a clue as to who it was. I also noticed that Q was not home yet. I pressed two on my phone to speed dial his number. He answered on the first ring and told me he was about to pull in the driveway. We hung up and a few minutes later he was walking in the bedroom door.

The next morning Q pulled into the airport parking lot. He paid the fare for us to park there for a week. I fell asleep on the airplane. When I woke up we were landing in Vegas. The cab driver took us to our hotel. We were staying at the Luxor.

I was amazed at our room. We had the tower premier suite. It had a king-sized bed, a breakfast nook, and a wet bar. It was 1,050 square feet. That is a nice size for a hotel. We decided to wind down for a few before we hit the town.

We hit the every store in the mall. I didn't buy something at every store, because I couldn't carry all that stuff on the plane. I had to hit up Victoria's Secret and Bath and Body Works. I also hit up BeBe. We caught a cab back to the hotel. We agreed to shower and then hit the casinos.

I looked over at Q on the slot machines. He was having a good time. I peeped him checking me out. I looked good regardless of me being four months pregnant.

# *Chapter 16*

## Q

I looked over at Neicee and she was looking back at me. She looked damn good to be four months pregnant. I was real happy right now. I was on cloud nine. A nigga put not one but two babies in her. I was trying to bid my time. I had the hotel set the room up for my proposal to her. I ordered rose petals and wine. I ordered all the seafood we could eat. Seafood was Neicee's favorite food. I loved her and I was ready to settle down with her.

When we walked in our room I looked over at Neicee. She had tears in her eyes. Rose petals led from the door to the bathroom. Rose petals were all on the bed. The food was laid out on the table.

"Wow Q. Did you do all this for me?" She said this while covering her mouth with tears still flowing. I kissed her on the forehead. She loves to be kissed on the forehead. I grabbed her hand and led her to the table. I wet a rag with soap and water and wiped her hands. We laughed and talked the whole dinner. I poured me a glass of Moët and her glass of the Welch's grape juice, the "wine" in the one bottle. I went over to the iPod dock and put on Boys II Men; that's her favorite old time group. As they were singing "On Bended Knee" I got down on one knee and proposed.

"Oh my God Q. Yes, I will marry you." She was jumping up and down with a big smile on her face. I looked in her eyes and I saw the love. I would never doubt her love for me again.

That night we made love like we never made it before. I laid her on the bed and I fucked her like my life depended on it.

"You wanted this dick? You better take it." She let her leg down. "Put your leg back up. You said you were going to get me, didn't you? Well get me then Neicee." I said all this to her while I watched her bite her lips like she did when she was having an orgasm. Her legs started to shake. She looked me in my eyes and whispered, "I'm Mrs. Dupree and this your pussy baby." I lost it. I nutted all over the sheets.

The next morning I heard Neicee on the phone with Na Na. She was telling her about the engagement. I went in the bathroom. I wasn't in the bathroom five minutes when Neicee burst in the door.

"Q they just arrested Tone for the murder of Ron." *Damn*, I said to myself. Nobody knew that Neicee killed Ron. I knew our trip was going to be cut short. I didn't want to disappoint Neicee. I knew she wouldn't mind because Tone was her friend too. I didn't have to say anything. She said she was calling the airline to see if she could get us an earlier flight.

# *Chapter 17*

## *Neicee*

We landed back in Charlotte and jumped in our car. I must admit I was a little upset. I didn't want my trip to end. I knew I had to represent Tone though. Q drove us to the police station on Spector Drive.

I went to the desk and let them know I was there for an attorney visit. She led me to the room and Tone was waiting on me. His whole face lit up when I walked in the room.

"Tell me what happened Tone. Why do they think you killed Ron?"

"They say I killed him on revenge. They don't even have a murder weapon. I didn't even know he was dead. I told those pigs I didn't kill him but I wanted to. Officer Kirklen punk ass got it out for me and Q for some reason. The funny part Neicee is he doesn't like you either." I looked at Tone. Him saying that let me know that Officer Kirklen was a dirty cop and he knew I was coming after his ass.

I left the police station and headed to the court house. I assured Tone he would be out by tonight. I was headed to get him a bond.

I left the court house and got back in the car with Q. I told him to head to Walkers Bonding. I called Na Na and told her Tone had a $20,000 bond and to meet us so she can bond him out.

I hugged Na Na when she walked in the door. I whispered in her ear that I had to tell her something later. We hadn't told anyone that I was having twins. I knew I also had to call my mom and brothers, but later. Now the focus was on bonding Tone out.

We left the bondsman's office. Q told Na Na to tell Tone to call him once he was released. She said she would and she got in her car. Q and I headed home.

Q pulled our bags out the car once we pulled in the garage. I was preparing for a shower when he walked in the bathroom.

"Sorry about the trip Neicee. I really wanted us to have that getaway."

It's okay baby. I know we had to get Tone out. I still got my ring," I said while smiling really hard. I wrapped my hair up and turned on the shower water. Q joined me in the shower.

I didn't put on any clothes when we got out the shower. I was horny as hell. I laid down on the bed spread eagle. I was playing with my pussy when Q walked in the room. I saw him licking his lips. I wanted to put on a show for him. I grabbed my rabbit out the nightstand beside the bed. I turned it on. I stuck it in my pussy and started rotating it around in circles. I then started pulling it in and out of my pussy. Q was about to go crazy. He loved to watch me play with myself. I then started pinching my left nipple while I summoned him with my other hand. He came closer. I pulled him to me. I pointed to the bed and told him to have a seat. I grabbed the chair from the vanity area and told him to sit in it. I went to the iPod deck and put on "Dance For You" by Beyoncé. I gave my baby a lap dance. As Beyoncé was saying "rocking on my babe" I was rocking on my babe for real. I had that nigga going crazy.

At the end of the song I told him to just keep sitting. I got on my knees and grabbed his dick. I flicked my tongue across the head of his dick. I then started to suck on the head of his dick like it was a blow pop. I was massaging his nuts while I was sucking on the head. I looked him in his eyes while I was doing all this. I knew that drove him crazy. I watched his eyes rolling. I put his whole dick in my mouth. I was sucking so hard my jaws looked like they were caving in.

Q laid me on the bed to return the favor. He pushed both of my legs back and stuck his tongue in my pussy. He licked one side then the other. He then tongue fucked my pussy. My legs started trembling. He ran his tongue up and down my pussy walls. He then started to suck on my pussy lips. By this time I was trembling really badly. My juices were flowing everywhere. I was sticky. I felt it all on my legs. That didn't stop Q. He started licking on my thighs. He gently put his dick in my pussy. He started rocking slowly. I had tears running down my face. It felt so good. He was real gentle and passionate. He rocked me slowly until we both burst a nut at the same time. Then we both dozed off.

I woke up to the sound of Q's cell phone playing Yo Gotti. I glanced at it and saw it was Tone. Q was knocked out. I didn't want to wake him, but I knew he would want to talk to Tone.

I woke Q up and put the phone in his hand.

"It's Tone," I told him.

"Hello. What's up man?" I couldn't really hear Tone's side of the story. I could only go off of what Q was saying.

"Tone and Na Na are coming over in a few. Put some clothes on." I jumped in the shower and put some shorts and a T-shirt on. While we were waiting on them I called my mom. She answered on the second ring.

"Hey Ma. I was calling to tell you that Q and I got engaged in Vegas." I heard the excitement in my mom's voice.

"You already know I am going to help you with this wedding. You're my only daughter."

"Ma that's not all. I am also pregnant with twins. I am having a boy and a girl."

"OMG." I heard my mom scream she was going to be a grandma. I am the youngest child my mom had, but I was blessing her with her first grandchildren. I chitchatted with my mom until I heard the doorbell ring. I knew it was Tone and Na Na.

"Hey diva," I said to Na Na when she walked in the door. We hugged and I hugged my goddaughter. We all headed outside to sit by the pool.

"Neicee that dirty ass cop Kirklen got it bad for you. I don't know what you did to that pig. The whole time he was asking me questions he kept bringing up your name. I told his punk ass to call and ask you." The whole time Tone was talking I glanced over at Q. I could tell he was mad as hell.

"What the fuck he asking about Neicee for? I don't want to kill no dirty ass cop but I will if he doesn't stop fucking with her."

"Well he arrested Mike last month. You know Mike, Tone. Black ass Mike from Grier Town. Well anyway he arrested him last month for a murder but he didn't have any evidence on Mike so I walked him out the police station myself. When Mike gets to my office he tells me that Officer Kirklen murdered Officer Hill over some drugs. Mike says he buys weight from both of them. Kirklen knows I am coming for his ass. After I solve this case I am running for D.A. Fuck all those dirty ass cops.

"Damn Neicee," Tone said. I didn't know you wanted to run for D.A."

"I don't but I will. Just to show them not to fuck with me."

Tone looked at me and Q.

"Well Q you better get ready. You already know some shit is going to go down. Neicee is stepping into a whole new league."

"I already know that Tone. Somebody has already been threatening her. This was going on before all of this though, so I don't think it is linked. Put your ears to the streets. My baby is pregnant. I will not let anything happen to her.

I looked over at Na Na. She wasn't saying anything. She always had something to say. "What's up Na Na? You are awful quiet."

"Nothing at all Neicee. I was just listening to y'all talk. I didn't know you wanted a response from me."

"I didn't, but you normally have something to say."

After Tone and Na Na left I went to bed. I was tired and I had a long day ahead of me. I had to find out what was up with Officer Kirklen.

The next morning Q left to go meet up with Tone. I called Los first. I told him the latest on what I knew about Officer Kirklen. I then called Mike. He picked up on the first ring. "What's up my favorite lawyer in the whole wide world?"

"I better be your only lawyer in the whole wide world," I said with the biggest grin on my face.

"You already know," Mike said to me.

"Mike I need you to tell me everything you need to know about Officer Kirklen. Now he is fucking with me. It just got personal."

I listened as Mike ran down everything he knew. Judges and all kind of powerhouse people were doing illegal shit. I mean I knew this kind of stuff went on. I just didn't know I was going to have to deal with it. I was going to blackmail Officer Kirklen. He was going to make this Ron shit disappear. I was tired of playing games with him. He was also going to leave Mike alone as well.

I got off the phone with Mike. I called Na Na to see if she wanted to go get something to eat. She said she had patients all day. I talked to her for a while and told her I was going to North Lake Mall. I was left by myself. I got dressed and hopped in the Escalade.

As I was leaving the mall I stepped into the parking lot. Out of nowhere a car hit me. I don't remember anything after that.

I woke up surrounded by people. The first thing I did was grab my stomach. I saw Q looking at me with tearful eyes. I started crying. My mom ran over and hugged me.

"Neicee calm down." That was my mom talking to me.

"The babies had to be delivered via emergency cesarean. It is kind of touch and go right now. They will make it baby. They have strong parents. They don't have a choice. I had Pastor Lauderdale here praying for my grandbabies."

"Ma you don't understand. Those are my kids. I loved them from the beginning when I first heard their heartbeats."

"Neicee you were losing a lot of blood. You have a broken leg and you had internal bleeding. Somebody was really trying to kill you."

"Neicee do you have a clue that did this to you?"
That was my oldest brother Lamont talking. I knew he
was upset and somebody was going to die. I was the
only girl. All five of my brothers were overprotective of
me.

"Lamont I don't know. I'm not a nasty person.
You already know that. All I do is go to work and come
home." My next to the oldest brother Damon looked at
Q.

"Somebody going to die. They tried to kill my
sister. We shutting Charlotte down tonight. Get your
crew and we will meet you at your house."

I knew my brothers were upset. I didn't want
things to get to far out of hand and everybody end up in

jail. My youngest brother Deveaux never said a word. He had always been the quiet one. He was also the most dangerous one out of all my brothers. I was wondering what was going through his mind. We were always the closest ones because we are only eleven months apart. He walked over and kissed me on my forehead. He whispered in my ear.

"I love you sis with everything in me, and somebody is going to die for this shit. I promise you on everything I love." He walked out the room. I knew Deveaux meant every word. He didn't broadcast what he was going to do. He said that to me for me. He was going to find out on his own what was going on.

Q was the last one to leave. "Neicee I am going to stop by neonatal and check on our babies. I am also going to pay Leeka a visit before I get up with your brothers. I want to make sure it wasn't her before I bring the heat to Ron's boys. They probably went after you because Ron is dead and they think Tone did it."

"Q please take me to the nursery with you. I have to see my kids." Q looked at me and told me he would be back.

Q came back into the room with a wheelchair. The nurse helped him get me in the chair. He wheeled me to the neonatal intensive care nursery. When he pushed me to the incubators I lost it. All I saw was my babies hooked up to all those machines. Q grabbed me and held me tight.

"It's going to be alright Neicee. We have to believe that."

"I know Q, but it hurts so much." A doctor came over as we were talking.

"Are you the parents?" We both shook our heads yes.

"Well the girl is a fighter. She is really holding on. She has a better chance than the boy but he is being strong too. We pulled the girl out first. She is bigger than her brother. She weighs two pounds. The boy weighs one pound seven ounces. If we can get the both of them breathing on their own then they will be alright. I looked at his badge before I called his name.

"Dr. Bell be honest with me. Do you feel like my babies have a chance? I don't want no sugarcoated shit. It will hurt like hell but I am a big girl.

"Ma'am I actually think your babies have a good chance of making it. It will be a long journey and it will be hard. I am not just telling you this." He walked off. I looked at Q.

"You can go handle your business. I want to be left alone. I want to spend some time with my babies. I will ask one of the nurses to take me back to my room."

Dr. Bell walked back over to us. He looked at me.

"Don't I know you? Your name is Neicee, right? You got a lot of brothers. Didn't you used to stay in Earl Village?" I looked at him.

"Yes, I remember you. You're Ru. You stayed across the parking lot from us. Look at you. A doctor, wow. You stayed in everything. I'm happy for you though."

"Oh don't get it twisted; I'm still crazy ass Ru," he said with a chuckle. I laughed. I told Q how crazy Ru was back in the day.

"Take care Neicee. I'm still real. I'm not going to shit you by telling you any lies." He walked out the nursery.

When I got back to my room my mom was there. I really didn't want to be bothered with anyone, but I knew my mom wasn't going anywhere. I prepared myself for the millions of questions I knew she was going to ask. She normally don't get in our business, but someone had crossed the line. They tried to take her baby girl out, and she didn't play that shit.

# Chapter 18

## Q

I went to North Charlotte. Leeka stayed on Union Street. She was walking in the house when I jumped out my car. I scared the shit out of her.

"Bitch I am going to kill your ass. You have fucked up fucking with Neicee. My babies in the hospital fighting for their lives." Without even thinking I grabbed that bitch by her throat.

"Q I swear I didn't bother Neicee. I just got back in town. You can ask my neighbors." For some reason I believed her. I let her neck go.

"Q tell Neicee to watch her circle. When I got up with you it was a setup. The whole pregnancy thing was a set up. I am pregnant, but the baby is not yours. I am leaving town. This is getting to be too much for me. Some woman approached me months ago and told me all about you. She paid me $10,000 to talk to you. She said I had to sleep with you in order to get paid. She told me her name was Asia, but I know that's not that bitch real name. Honestly Q no offense, but I really don't care enough about you to be going through all this. I thought I saw the girl with Tone, but I'm not sure. I couldn't figure out why someone in your circle would be after the two of you. All I can say is just watch your circle. I am leaving Charlotte. You don't have to ever worry about me again."

"Are you trying to tell me Tone is out to get me?"

"No that's not what I'm saying. Some bitch is out to get Neicee is what I'm saying. Neicee was her focus the whole time. All she kept saying is she wanted her to hurt. She said Neicee hurt her, and she was going to pay big time."

"Leeka do you think this woman did this to Neicee or do you think one of Ron's boys did this?"

"Honestly Q I don't know. It could have been either or. I did warn Ron that Neicee was your girl. I didn't want him to do anything to her, but I was mad at how y'all was trying to play me. I don't know if Ron did it or had someone do it." I looked at Leeka. She obviously didn't know Ron was dead the way she was talking.

"Leeka did you not know that Ron was dead?" She had a shocked look on her face.

"No Q I didn't know that. I just got back to town when you saw me. I been in Miami. I'm moving there."

"Thanks Leeka." I walked back to my car.

I called Tone to get his take on what Leeka was talking about. We both were puzzled as to who this woman was. I told Tone to meet me at my house with the crew. I knew shit had just got real. Neicee's brothers were no joke. If they said we were shutting the city down tonight then that's exactly what we were going to do. Her oldest brother Lamont's name had been ringing in the streets. He just kept to his self. If you didn't fuck with him or anybody he loved then you was cool with him. Lamont was the truth.

Lamont was already waiting on me when I pulled up. I let the garage up and told him to pull in. He already had a different car. He said he would go over the plan once everyone got there. I told him about my beef with Ron. He said he was already one up on me. He knew where those niggas laid their heads and that's where we were going.

Once everyone got there Lamont went over the plans. Ron's crew stayed on Allen Street in North Charlotte. We wasn't taking the whole crew. We didn't need everybody. We agreed for Lamont, Tone, and me to ride out. I looked at Neicee's youngest brother Deveaux. He was too quiet. I knew he wanted to ride out too. He was the closest to Neicee out of all her brothers.

"Deveaux do you want to go?" I asked him. He shook his head yes. We jumped in the car and sped off.

It was quiet on Allen Street when we got there. It was a little too quiet if you asked me. Something just didn't seem right. As soon as we passed the store on the corner of Allen and Belmont I heard a loud pop. It was a gunshot. Those fools were already waiting on us. Deveaux jumped out the car with an AS59 sniper rifle. Where this nigga got that gun from I did not know. That was one of the most dangerous weapons in the world. He blew the nigga's whole head off. I knew that nigga was crazy when he spit on the dead body and jumped back in the car. He didn't say a word. Before we could drive off I spotted another nigga peeking his head from behind a car. I pumped nine bullets in his chest. I emptied my whole clip. First rule: never leave a witness. By this time we heard sirens. We didn't know which way they were coming from. We had to get out the car. We wasn't going to make it and we knew it.

We all got out the car and went our separate ways. I saw Lamont wiping off our fingerprints. The car was stolen so other than our prints they couldn't link the car to us. I wiped my gun and threw it in the sewer. I wasn't half way down the street when I heard "freeze." I threw my hands in the air.

"You black fucker, you better not move. Turn around slowly." I did as I was told. By this time people were coming outside. We was in the hood so I knew they was coming to be nosey. The white cop calmed down once he realized he had a crowd. His backup pulled up.

They began to question me about the shooting. Then Officer Kirklen's dumb ass pulled up.

"Q what you doing over here boy?"

"I didn't know I couldn't come over here boy," I said back to his punk ass.

"You can go where you want to go, true, but this isn't your neighborhood. Where is your car?"

"Look Kirklen. Arrest me if that's what you're going to do or let me go. I don't have to answer any of your questions. Just like you said I am free to go where I please. I was just being nice. Do I need to call my lawyer?" He started laughing.

He walked closer to me.

"We both know somebody tried to kill your bitch, so don't play." I wanted to murder his punk ass right there. He saw the hate in my eyes. I thought to myself, *On everything I love I'm going to kill his punk ass.*

"Let him go boys," he told the other cops as he walked off.

I walked to Siegel Avenue. I had a cousin that stayed on that street. I called Tone to see if he was okay. Him picking up the phone let me know that he was. I told him to meet me at the crib. I gave my cousin $50 to take me home. She only drove a Honda Civic. I knew it didn't cost that much in gas, but I was thankful for her time.

I wasn't expecting to see anybody at my house. The only person I was expecting was Tone. He was right behind me. He must have had somebody take him to his car. He knew better than to let anybody know where I laid my head. I shut and locked the door behind him.

"Q where the hell did your brother-in-law's crazy ass get that gun from? That nigga is crazy as hell. I didn't know he had that in him."

"You know how close he is to his sister man. I saw it in his eyes. He was going to kill everything moving fucking with Neicee. Well Tone, let me head back to the hospital. I got to check on my babies. Tone I'm a father. Damn, it feels good to say that shit. I got me two babies."

"Did you know she was having twins Q? Now your family is complete. You got your twin nines and now your twins." He was laughing when he said it, so I knew he was being funny.

"Yes I knew. We hadn't really had a chance to tell anybody yet. Oh yeah, before I forget let me tell you what punk ass Officer Kirklen said."

After I told Tone what he said he left.

I went straight to the nursery to see my babies. I washed my hands in the sink they had in there. I just stood over the incubator looking at them. I stuck my hand in the hole to rub their arms. They were so tiny. I instantly said a silent prayer. I begged God to let my babies make it. I knew it would crush Neicee if they didn't make it. The whole Charlotte was going to die if my babies didn't survive. I didn't even wanted to entertain that thought.

I walked in Neicee's room and overheard Na Na asking her if she had come up with names for the babies. She told her yes but she wasn't naming them. Na Na asked her why and she said she didn't think they were going to make it anyway. They didn't notice I was in the room. I went over and sat on the bed beside Neicee. I hugged her tight.

"Baby don't you ever think that. Our babies got strong genes. They are going to make it."

It tore me up to see my baby like that. She looked like she didn't have any fight in her. I didn't know who I was looking at. That was not the Neicee I knew. I kissed her on the forehead and told her I would be right back.

I went to the gift shop. I bought 'it's a boy' and 'it's a girl' balloons, pens, and buttons. I also bought a 'congratulations mom' balloon and cigars. I bought Neicee some roses. I had to cheer my baby up. I took all that back to her room. Her face lit up when I came into the room. It made me feel good to see her smile.

"Thank you so much baby. This means a lot to me." There was a lot I had to tell Neicee, but now was not the time. Na Na was in the room, and at this point I didn't trust anybody but Tone and Neicee. It was nothing personal to Na Na, but she was Neicee's friend first. I only talked to her because of Tone and Neicee.

"What's up Na Na?" I walked over and gave her a hug. She hugged me extra tight for some reason. I didn't think anything else of it.

"What's up Q? Congratulations on the twins. I'm an aunty." She walked over and hugged Neicee.

"Girl I'm going to get up out of here. Call me later."

After Na Na left I sat beside Neicee on the bed.

"I went to the nursery and checked on the kids. They are so beautiful. I'm a daddy Neicee. I know some things got to change in my life."

As I was telling Neicee everything that went down Na Na walked back into the room.

"I forgot my cell phone." As she was picking up her phone Channel 9 Eyewitness News did a breaking story.

"This just in, we have a double murder on Allen Street in North Charlotte. Police are on the scene and they have no suspects. No names have been released until the family has been notified." Na Na turned and looked at me. She didn't say anything to me though. She just waved and walked back out the door.

"What was that about?" Neicee asked me. I shook my head and told her I didn't know.

I finished telling Neicee what all had went down. We both were wondering who this mysterious woman was.

"Well Neicee I think we should go ahead and give our babies their names. You already know that's my junior right there so don't trip." I was smiling big as I was saying this. We decided on Quinton Demon

Dupree, Jr. and Quintina Shaneice Dupree. Neicee said the birth certificate lady would be back in the morning. I fell asleep on the couch.

Throughout the night nurses were in and out the room. I couldn't get any sleep. I was back and forth to the nursery checking on my babies. They were doing fine.

As promised the birth certificate lady came bright and early. We gave her the names and she said I had to sign because we weren't married yet. I was happy to sign. I had a surprise baby shower planned for Neicee when she got out the hospital. She didn't really fool with too many females but she still had some of the girls she grew up with that she still talked to. I also invited her favorite cousin Lashonda. Lashonda had gotten married a few years ago and Neicee was trying to let her have her space. I didn't understand it because I knew she missed her cousin. She told me that once before.

After the lady left I pushed Neicee in a wheelchair to the nursery. She wanted to see the babies. We washed up at the sink and walked over to the incubator. She rubbed Quinton Jr's leg and I rubbed Quintina's leg. I grabbed Neicee's other hand and we prayed as a family. Dr. Bell came over and talked to us. He said our babies were showing progress. That made me feel good inside.

I pushed Neicee back to her room. Denise was waiting in the room when we got there. "I wanted to see my grandbabies, but they said only two at a time. I didn't want to interrupt y'all, so I just waited."

"You can go back Ma."

"Oh yeah," she said. "The detective came by. He said the tags on the car was stolen, so he doesn't know who was driving the car. All he know is it was a female." She walked out the room. She walked out and Deveaux walked in. He walked over and kissed his sister on the cheek.

"Can I see my niece and nephew?"

"Catch Mom. She is on her way to see them.

"My sister is a mother. Oh Lord," he said as he walked out the room.

"When are they going to let you go home? This couch is uncomfortable and the nurses be in and out. I didn't get any sleep last night." Neicee was laughing at me.

"Poor baby," she said. I thumped her on the arm.

"Baby I been doing some thinking. I am trying to figure out how to invest. I think my best bet is to buy some trucks. I want to buy like three 18-wheeler trucks. I got to be around to raise my kids."

"I will probably go home tomorrow. Go home and get you some rest. Come back later on tonight."

When I got in the car I immediately got on the phone. I had to do some last minute preparations. Na Na was helping me, but I really wanted to do it myself. I had rented a ballroom at the Hilton in University. I had to call them to give them a final date. I had Sylvia's on Beatties Ford Road doing the food. I had called her cousin Frankie, who owned a bakery called BW Sweets. He was located in Cornelius, NC. He was a fool with his cakes. I could not take that from him.

I pulled my car into the garage and went into the house. My phone went off, letting me know I had a text message. It was from Leeka.

Leeka: *Q I got a picture of that bitch that I was telling you about. My phone messed up right now. Can't send picture mail. As soon as I get a replacement I will send u the picture.*

My face lit up like a Christmas tree. This was the first break we'd had. I texted her back.

Q: *okay I really appreciate this.*

I got in the shower and laid down. I had a lot on my mind.

# *Chapter 19*

## *Neicee*

I heard my phone alert going off. I reached for my phone. It was a text message.

Unknown: *Damn bitch I hate I didn't kill your ass.*

It didn't even bother me anymore. Then my work phone rang. It was an unknown call. I knew it was Peanut. My whole mood changed.

"Hello," I said into the phone.

"Hey Ne Ne. You been on my mind real hard. Have you been okay?"

I poured my heart out to Peanut. I was always able to talk to him. He was a friend. I also gave him the address to my condo downtown to give to his parole officer. I knew he was coming home soon and needed a place to lay his head. Peanut didn't have much family. His mom died when we was teenagers. That's why he took to the streets young. He had to raise his little sister. She was 14 years younger than us. I had been slipping lately. I used to check on her to make sure she was straight. I'd been knowing her all her life and I was the only sister she knew. I told Peanut I couldn't get around that much, but I would make sure he got some clothes. I was going to ask Shannon, my legal secretary, if she would do it for me. We hung up the phone.

I pressed the button for the nurses' station.

"Can someone come help me get my life together?" I heard the lady laugh. I knew she didn't know what I meant so I was laughing too. "That means I need to take a shower and stuff."

"Oh okay Ms. Love. I will send someone right in. I'm going to have to use that. I like that saying. It's cute."

Shortly after, my nurse assistant walked in. Her badge read Shondell. I made small talk with her. I didn't meet any strangers. I could make friends anywhere. After Shondell left Dr. Breamer walked in my room. She did a brief examination. She pulled a chair up beside the bed.

"Shaneice how are you feeling? When I say this I'm asking about mentally as well as physically. You have been through some things these past few days."

"Dr. Breamer honestly I feel fine. I was feeling sad at first, but I got a good support system.

"Well do you want to go home today? I will clear you on the OB side. I know it's going to be rough with your leg being broken in so many places." She told me she needed to see me back in her office in six weeks, and walked out the door.

I was hoping no one else came in. I wanted some time to myself before Q came back. I had a lot on my mind. I had to think positive. I was going to get someone to come in and finish up my nursery. I was putting them in the same room until they turned one. I was going to do pink and yellow. Yellow was Q's favorite color. I decided I may just do the whole room yellow. Yellow was a mutual color. I wasn't really sure how long my babies would have to stay in the hospital, but I was going to be ready when they did come home.

I made a few calls to various people. I talked to all my brothers and my mom. I talked to Q for a few minutes and told him I was being released today. I saved Na Na for last. I knew I was going to need Na Na once I got home.

"What's up diva?" she said when she answered.

"Na Na you know I am going to need some help when I get home. I know I can count on my best friend."

"You already know I got you Neicee. I don't even know why you asked."

"Well Q is on his way to get me. They are releasing me today. I'm going to go crazy sitting at home while my babies are here." We chatted it up for a few minutes and we got off the phone.

After I got off the phone with Na Na I began to pray. Killing Ron was heavy on my mind. I prayed God didn't let my babies suffer because I killed Ron. I never spoke to Q about it, but it was starting to bother me. I snapped out of it real quick when Q walked in the room.

"Are you ready to go home?" I shook my head yes as I pushed the call button to let my nurse know my ride was here. The nurse came in and brought me my discharge papers. I told Q I wanted to see our babies before I left. He said he already knew that. He pushed me to the nursery.

There were doctors all around our baby's incubator when we walked in. I immediately began to panic. The nurse walked over to inform us that they were fine. The doctor had called in his team to check the babies out. They were trying to see how much their lungs had developed because they are on ventilators. I breathed a sigh of relief.

Dr. Bell walked over to talk to us.

"We ran some tests on your babies today. They are progressing fine. I want them to be at least four pounds and breathing on their own before I will let them go home. They are gaining weight pretty fast. They are on the right track. The nurse informed me that you have been pumping breast milk. That is the best thing you can do. Once they start feeding breast milk is very healthy for your babies. Feel free to bring in family pictures to put on the incubator. Make your babies feel your presence. You can talk to them. They know you are here."

"Thank you Dr. Bell," we both said at the same time. He walked out with his team. Q and I stayed a long time. We took turns reading to them. One of the nurses took our picture. She had a Polaroid camera. She taped the picture to the incubator. We said a prayer and we left.

I noticed Q was not headed to the house.

"Where are we going?"

"Just trust me Neicee. I got to make a stop." The next thing I knew we were pulling up at the University Hilton.

"Q I really want to go home." I got to meet somebody real quick Neicee and I don't want to leave you in the car."

Q helped me out the car. The hospital sent me home with a wheelchair, so he pulled it out the back of our Escalade. He pushed me to the elevator. We went down. When we got off the elevator all I saw was 'new mom' banners and 'congratulations' balloons. I was so happy. I looked at Q and said thank you. I looked around the room and all my childhood friends were there. My favorite cousin Lashonda was there. I missed her. I was so glad she was there. All my brothers were there and of course my mom. I saw Na Na putting gifts on the gift table. She looked good. She had on a pair of Michael Kors Jeans and a bright red blouse. She had on a pair of bright red Steve Madden heels and the accessories to match. She looked up and saw me. She hugged me tight.

"What's up diva?" she said as she told Q where to place me. My cousin Lashonda walked over and gave me a hug.

The baby shower was going great. We played a lot of games. Some of the games involved questions about me and Q.

"It's time to open up the gifts." That was my mom talking.

"These are my first grandkids. Neicee is the only daughter I have. I know she is well off and can buy whatever she wants to for her kids but her brothers and I wanted to show her how much we love her. Everybody bought their own separate gifts that they wanted to present to their sister. My oldest Lamont wants to go first and then the rest of her brothers will go. After we are finished everyone else can fall in."

My brother Lamont bought me two baby swings. My brother Damon bought me the twin stroller and matching car seats. My brother Deveaux bought me two bouncers. My brother Ricky bought two baby bathtubs and two bottle Warmers. Jason gave me two

$1,000 Visa gift cards. He said he would just let me buy what they needed later on. My mom bought two cribs, and a Winnie the Pooh crib set. I was in tears. I didn't have to buy anything. I had so many diapers of all sizes. Clothes of all sizes. Na Na said she had the nursery done for me as a gift. I was outdone.

When we got home Q pushed me to the nursery. He wanted me to see what Na Na had done to the room. It was so beautiful. I saw why my mom bought Winnie the Pooh. Na Na had decorated the room with it. She had the walls painted in the colors of Winnie the Pooh. The baby's names were painted on the wall. I didn't know what to say. I knew I was loved.

Q helped me wash up and get my night clothes on. I knew I was going to go crazy. I didn't like feeling helpless. My leg was messed up pretty bad. The physical therapist wasn't able to start until next week. My leg was broken in three different places. I was told not to put any pressure on it. I was glad it was my left leg and not my right. If push came to shove I could still drive. I also thank God for Na Na. I loved my best friend. It was nice to have a doctor for a best friend.

We were lying in the bed flipping channels and talking.

"Q I feel so elated. So many people showed up to show us love. Some people I hadn't seen in years. I was so happy to see Lashonda. She made me promise to keep in touch. I just be wanting her to have her space. She got a good man this time. I love him for her."

"Oh yeah Neicee while I'm thinking about it, Leeka sent me a text message." I couldn't miss the look on Neicee's face.

"Actually it isn't what you thinking Neicee. She told me she got a picture of the girl, but her phone messed up right now. It won't let her send pictures. She will send it as soon as she get her phone together."

At that moment Q's phone rang. It was Tone. He picked up and talked to him. I heard him ask him if he was okay with him mentioning it to me. Tone must have said yes.

"Neicee, Tone seems to think it may have been Maya. He says Leeka saw him with her."

"One thing I do know is that I'm on everybody's hit list right now. The crazy part is I don't even know why. Q I ain't never been a nasty person. I'm sweet

Neicee. I ain't never took no shit and I can get dirty

with the rest of them, but I will give my shirt off my

back. I'm confused as to what's going on."

I reached for my phone to call the hospital to check

on my babies. The nurse said they were doing fine. I

laid my head on Q's chest and we fell asleep like that.

The next morning I woke up to Na Na calling me.

She was letting me know she was about to pull up. Q

went and let her in. I heard him telling her he

appreciated her coming over, but he could handle it. Na

Na told him I was her best friend and she wouldn't have

it any other way.

# Chapter 20

## Q

I watched as Na Na went up the stairs to our bedroom. They had been friends as long as I had been friends with Tone. Na Na always hung around us, but that was because she was Neicee's friend. Tone was my friend so he hung around as well. We knew they liked each other, because they used to flirt. When Tone told me Na Na was pregnant I was shocked. I didn't even know they had hooked up for real. For some reason that was a secret Tone kept from me. He just kept saying she was different from the other women he dated. She was wifey material. I wasn't sure why he never wifed her. Their daughter was three years old. I also didn't know why he insisted on staying in the hood. I would never have Neicee in the hood like that. Na Na was a

doctor, and Tone had plenty of money. He could afford

to move. Not to mention that Na Na had a condo

downtown just like Neicee did. Tone insisted on

staying off West Blvd. Don't get me wrong, their house

was real nice, but I'm just saying. Well it wasn't any of

my business I guess, but I was going to ask him.

I heard Na Na yell my name from upstairs. I went

to the intercom and pressed the button.

"What's up Na Na?"

"Q I left my pocketbook and phone in my car. Can

you get it for me?"

"Come on Na Na. You know I don't want to be

bothered with your purse. You and your friend don't

carry purses. Y'all carry suitcases." I was laughing as I walked out to my driveway. Na Na's phone was ringing. I couldn't help but to notice the caller. The caller ID showed Ham as the caller. The only Ham I knew was one of Ron's boys. I started laughing. Tone was out here thinking Na Na wasn't doing anything. These women were tired of us. I knew I had to say something though, because Na Na was sleeping with the enemy and I didn't want her to get hurt. I was going to say something to Na Na though.

I walked back into the house. I pushed the intercom button and told Na Na to come downstairs. When she walked in the room I went in on her.

"Look Na Na what you do is your business, but you're barking up the wrong tree. When I was getting your phone out the car I saw Ham call you."

Her whole facial expression changed. I hushed her before she got started.

"All I'm saying is Ham is not our friend. I don't want you to get hurt. Whatever you're doing with him this shit stops today. Tone will kill that nigga and you too. You know he will." I walked off. Na Na went back upstairs.

I was sitting outside by the pool when my friend with the car dealer's license called. I told him to see if he could find me three 18-wheelers. I had one major drug deal left with some Mexicans. It was going to bring me $5 million. I was leaving the game after that. I was passing the baton to Tone. I wished he would leave the game with me. He had enough money to retire and still live a good life.

"Tell me something good Reico. Please tell me you found me at least one truck."

"I did even better Q. I found you three like you wanted. I found you a 2009 Volvo with a full cab. I also found you two 2012 freightliners with the full cab. For all three trucks you're looking at about $70,000 dollars. I will fax you the paperwork. You can have Neicee look at it if you want to."

I hung up the phone. I was happy. Everything was falling into place. Once I figured out who this woman was my life was going to be normal.

I walked in on Neicee telling Na Na that we wasn't going to get married until the babies came home, but she was going to plan it. She said she didn't have anything else to do, because she was out of work for a while. Na Na told her she would help her.

"Neicee I'm going to ride out for a few. Call me when you're ready to go see our babies." I kissed her on the forehead and walked out the room.

I had just hopped on the highway and I spotted Officer Kirklen. I checked my secret compartment in my car to make sure I had my 45. He didn't even see me. I followed his ass. He was a dirty ass cop. I watched him make plenty of drug transactions. I really didn't care though because this was his last day breathing. I was going to kill his ass today.

"What the hell?" I said to myself as I watched him pull into a two-level mini mansion off Providence

Road. This nigga must've known something I didn't. How the hell could he afford this shit off a cop's salary? That let me know right there he had some higher ups involved too. I was coming back for his ass tonight. I was the nigga that would be sitting on your bed waiting on you to get out the shower. I pulled off. I went to the hood.

Little Rock Apartments were quiet. It wasn't too much going on other than the kids out playing. The ice cream truck pulled up. I handed the ice cream man $200 dollars.

"Give these kids what they want." I yelled out to the kids to get them some ice cream. All the kids ran to the truck. I knew the ice cream man was probably going to leave after that.

I got back in my car and pulled off. I headed towards South Side Apartments to see what was jumping over there. I drove down Baltimore and saw Tonya. I used to fuck Tonya back in the day before I met Neicee. Tonya was bad as hell. She put you in mind of Lisa Raye. Tonya looked bad as hell now. She was on that powder bad. I didn't know how she got like that. She was very strong minded. Word on the street was that it was that nigga Roc she used to mess with. They say he used to beat her ass. She used that powder as an escape. I had always heard there was a story behind every addiction. I'm not sure if it is true or not. I never tried anything. I didn't even smoke weed. It was a few other people out. I spoke to Ray Ray and Dula. I drove out of the neighborhood. I decided to sweep through Brook Hill. I drove up Brook Hill road. Tay and Lela were outside doing what they did best. They'd been together forever. All they did was get drunk and argue. I respected them though. Through all the bullshit they were still together. I headed back to the house.

# *Chapter 21*

## Q

When I got back to the house Na Na was gone. I went to our room to see if Neicee was there. She wasn't in our room either. I hit the intercom button to call her over the house. She responded that she was in the nursery. I went to her.

"Why didn't you call me when Na Na left? I told you I would take you to the hospital so we can see the kids."

"I know Q. She just left, but I'm ready to go whenever you are."

# Neicee

Dr. Bell was there when we arrived at the hospital.

"What's up fool?" he said to me. I just laughed. He used to always say that when we were growing up. His mom would tell him that's a sin. He would tell her not go there with the spiritual tip. I remember he told her as long as he smoked cigarettes not to come at her about anything being a sin. He wasn't disrespectful but that's what he meant.

"Your babies are doing wonderful. I'm happy about their progress." Q was smiling at the news.

We visited the babies for a while. I pumped some breast milk. We said a prayer and we left.

"Neicee will you be okay for a little while at the house by yourself? I have a few errands to run. I will stop by Showmars and get you something to eat."

I shook my head yes. Q went to the Showmars on 7th Street, the one by Carolinas Medical Center Mercy.

Q

I got Neicee situated at the house. I drove back to South Side. I needed a car. When I got there my old friend Jake was standing outside. He was just the man I needed to see. He could get you anything, from a house to a car. Nothing was too big or too small for Jake. I pulled up beside him and told him what I needed. He told me to relax for about an hour and he had me. I stayed around and waited on the call from Jake. He finally called. He had me a stolen car. I parked my car in Wilmore at Na Na's sister Jazz house. I grabbed my bag out the trunk. I had to put on my all-black clothes. After I was dressed I drove the car to Officer Kirklen's house.

When I got to his house I went around back to turn the power off in his house. Being a street nigga I knew he was going to come outside to investigate. When he came outside I was going to be waiting on him.

I heard the front door open. I waited on him to come off the porch. He was on his cell phone when I walked up behind him. I pulled out my scalpel and called his name. I wanted him to know I was going to kill him and why I was going to kill him.

"Officer Kirklen I don't take threats lightly. You breathed Neicee's name out your mouth. For that today is your last day breathing." With that being said, I sliced his throat, and when I made sure that he was indeed dead, I walked to the car like nothing even happened.

*To be continued!*

CPSIA information can be obtained at www.ICGtesting.com
Printed in the USA
LVOW10s0012160416

483815LV00025B/529/P

Take a ride down the streets of Charlotte NC, be‍
known as the Queen city. Shaneice, also known
Neicee and her boyfriend Quentin, known as Q ta‍
you on a whirlwind of surprises.

Q loves Neicee with everything in him, but he c‍
remain faithful to her. Neicee is from the hood‍
grew up the only girl of 6 kids. She was determine‍
never go back to where she came from. Des‍
where she's from, she graduated from law school‍
has built the reputation of the baddest hood law
to ever grace the streets of Charlotte. Now, some
is out to kill her. Could it one of Q's side pieces?

Unbeknownst to Q, Neicee has her own secrets.‍
he lose her? You will have to read it to see if she
remain the ride or die chick he has grown to love‍

# SHMEL CARTE‍

ISBN 9781530883592

9 781530 883592